MERMAID OF SICILY

MERMAID OF VENICE: BOOK TWO

JINCEY LUMPKIN

ABOUT THE AUTHOR

JINCEY LUMPKIN is a writer who splits her time between NYC and Lisbon. She has been profiled by Dateline NBC, *Vice*, and *GQ*, among others. *Out* Magazine listed her in its "OUT 100", naming her as one of the world's most influential LGBTQ+ people, alongside celebrities like Laverne Cox and Ricky Martin.

For access to exclusive excerpts from Jincey's upcoming books and invites to live readings, visit JINCEYLUMPKIN.COM and join the Insider Circle email list.

facebook.com/jinceylumpkin

twitter.com/jinceylumpkin

instagram.com/storiesbyjincey

To request permissions, contact the publisher at jincey@jinceylumpkin.com

Ebook: 978-1-7364712-1-0
Hardcover: 978-1-7376155-1-4
Paperback: 978-1-7376155-0-7

CIP Block/Library of Congress Number: 1-10686057179

First edition July 2021.

Edited by Amanda E. Clark
Cover art by Jason Brooks
Cover art direction by Matthew Axe
Cover layout by Lauren Balistreri

For my beautiful wife, Eva.

Two crooked teeth
is my lover,
black curls, strong hands
different and the same are we

Grief has my lover
hard heart, heavy thoughts
Pain makes distance
I her, she me

Warm arms is my lover
a whisper, a whip
Brown eyes close together
a sigh, a sigh

ACKNOWLEDGMENTS

I want to send a big thank you out to my author buddies. Whether I know you from "real life" or whether we met on Clubhouse or Instagram, you have been a huge source of comfort and support. A special shoutout to Melissa Chambers and the Romance Writers Marketing Group, Lucy Goodchild, Joe Solari, Kimani Lauren, Chris Rackliff, Tom Dumbrell, Harper Glenn, and Satia Renee. Selling books is hard! I had no idea how hard it was until I embarked on my self-publishing journey. You all have helped me learn years of lessons in mere months, and for that, I am so grateful.

To my friends, family, and readers, thank you for buying my books, for reading them, and for passing them on. I remain ever grateful. It is for you that I write!

Thank you to Matthew Axe for your guidance, not only on branding and design, like the cover of this beautiful book, but also in life. You are a dear friend and beloved confidant.

Amanda, thank you for your brilliant editing, as always. My ideas often feel absolutely crazy, but when you co-sign, I know I'm on the right track.

TRIGGER WARNING

This book contains intense descriptions of violence and abuse, including sexual abuse, murder, and torture.

MERMAID OF SICILY

1

Christmas Eve

"**M**erry Fucking Christmas," Harper mumbled to herself. Her brother's body had been pulled out of the water and was now lying in a body bag that had been placed at the very edge of the Rio di Cannaregio. Considering the situation, Harper knew that any normal person would cry, would show emotion. Her father and mother certainly were. Leaning on one another, Bronwyn and Royce embraced, letting the first of many tears rush out.

But Harper felt nothing except a cold rage, so cold in fact, that the frigid air whipping through the canals hit her cheeks and bounced right off.

There was only one thing that sparked a bit of warmth in Harper's dark heart: making Gia pay for killing Cameron.

2

December 20th—Before Dawn

The iron bars on the exterior gate clanged in the darkness as Cameron fumbled to escape. Gia tiptoed along the wall, feeling her way toward him. Her emotions wove as erratically as cars on a busy highway. Desire: wanting Cam to stay and yet wanting to drain the life from his body. Arousal: The thought of cutting him open excited her, and she could feel the skin separating on her arms as her gills emerged. There was sadness, too, because she knew that once she cut him, he'd be gone for good, and she was sure now more than ever that she loved him.

The lock clicked open and the door swung out as Cameron bolted onto the street. Light from the canal flooded Gia's courtyard, and instinctively, she retreated into the shadows. Outside, one reporter yelled at Cameron, then another. Camera flashes captured photos of him as he ran from Gia's palazzo. Gia shrank along the wall until she reached the gate. She hid herself behind the wood but reached an arm out, slamming the gate closed, locking it. Screaming her name, the hungry press all wanted their bite of the Mermaid of Venice. Over the courtyard, a drone buzzed and hovered, seeking Gia with its prying glass eye. She hurried inside and seemingly barricaded herself in, turning her back against the door as if actively holding off an intruder.

Why did Cameron have to run off like that?

If he'd just listened, she would have explained to him why she had her mother's bones in her home. He should not have fled from her. But his fear had gotten the better of him, and now everyone knew where Gia was, and there was nothing she could do about it.

Perhaps *La Nonna* could help.

Gia dialed her lawyer from the burner phone that had been purchased in Serbia on the way back to Venice. *La Nonna* sounded groggy, but she answered.

Gia's voice trembled as she spoke. "I need you to come to Venice immediately."

"Good morning to you, Gia. What a pleasant way to wake up an old woman. How are you? Have you killed your boyfriend? Such a shame if you have. He seemed like a very nice young man."

3

The Langleys hustled through Marco Polo airport. Just after passing through customs, they were greeted by two men: the mayor of Venice and its *Capo della Polizia*, the Chief of Police. Harper was impressed, although she didn't let it show; apparently, Royce and Bronwyn had wasted no time in liaising directly with the bigwigs. They were received like VIPs should be. The mayor's personal zero-emissions-hybrid boat ferried the three Langleys to their hotel.

"We're desperate," Bronwyn's voice was steady, but only because she was making a concerted effort to keep it so. "We haven't heard from our son in almost three weeks."

"He is a grown man, no?" the mayor replied.

Il Capo sat back with his arms crossed, his captain's hat strangling the thick skin around his forehead. "I do not think one can expect a man to call his mamma every day. My own son, ha! We are lucky if we hear from him twice in one year."

"Darling," Bronwyn said to her husband, placing a hand on his arm. "Show them."

Royce unzipped his leather messenger bag and pulled out a large iPad. He flicked through news stories as well as recently-captured press photos of Cameron fleeing Gia's palazzo.

"These are from this morning," Royce explained. "And... so is this." Royce clicked on a time-stamped security video from inside Gia's house. In the footage, Cameron held a large bone and was seen backing away from Gia, as if he had been terrified.

"Is that..." the mayor interrupted Bronwyn and slid two fingers across the screen, zooming into the footage.

"It is Gia Acquaviva!" *Il Capo*'s mouth dropped. "Your son was with the Mermaid?"

Bronwyn snatched the iPad from Royce. "Yes," she replied to the Italians, "they have been seeing each other since September. We believe she was holding him hostage. I want my son found, and she knows where he is. You have to bring her in for questioning."

The two men began whispering to each other in Italian. Harper listened intently to try to pick up what they were saying, but despite her time in Venice earlier in the year covering the disappearance and then the murder of Nicolás Ángel Fernández, her Italian was still atrocious. Admittedly, Harper was a bit jealous of her father's influence. In all her months working in Venice, she had not managed to make it all the way up the chain of command within the police force. She felt bitter that her father could have easily pulled out the big guns out for her, and she wondered why he hadn't.

"Pardon me, gentlemen," Royce interrupted what he felt was probably idle gossip to try and keep the Italians on track. "We have collected quite a bit of evidence on Miss Acquaviva. We think some of it may be relevant to another open investigation."

Il Capo frowned. Arched in an unnaturally irksome shape, his eyebrows resembled thick caterpillars. "Excuse me, Mr. Langley, but when it concerns the American media, we have our reservations. Is it not the American media that have pushed us all into this perilous 'post-truth' world? A man of authority, like myself? I prefer unadulterated facts. There is always one truth... not 'versions' of it. I have dedicated my life to making a separation between the facts and the fiction all you so-called journalists love to sell."

"What are you saying? That you won't look at this other evidence?" Royce shook his leather bag, rustling its contents.

One of *Il Capo*'s eyebrows was raised high, while the other twitched. "Evidence of what exactly?"

"Murder!" Royce screeched.

As if on cue with the tension of the moment, the wooden speed-boat jerked abruptly and they all slid in their seats. The driver hopped off to tie the boat to the pier at the Hotel Bauman. The mayor took Bronwyn's age-dappled hand and stroked it, whispering to her. "We will do everything we can for you, Mamma. And, *Signor* Langley, I will speak to my friend the captain in private." He stood and slapped *Il Capo* on the back, "I do not know about this old one here, but I would very much like to see anything that you have regarding *Signorina* Acquaviva."

The hotel concierge and two security guards smuggled the Langleys through a side entrance. As the family passed the threshold into the dark, it appeared as though a giant marble beast had swallowed them whole.

4

December 20th—Early Afternoon

The din of the photographers and reporters screaming
outside of Gia's palazzo was maddening and constant—it
was enough to give her tinnitus. This was precisely the kind
of circumstance she'd always done her best to avoid. Thanks to the
buzzy little drones, she couldn't even go into her own courtyard,
which also meant she couldn't slip out into the canals via the secret
hatch in her pool. Suffice to say, Gia felt trapped.

In addition to the intense media hubbub at her doorstep, Gia
found herself worrying about Cameron. Was he out there talking to
the press? Talking to Harper? Would she turn on the TV to see
footage of the inside of her own living room? Was Harper glaring into
her cell phone at that moment, watching Gia even now?

Gia regretted leaving Harper's spy cameras up. It had been a
serious miscalculation. She had strategized—and believed in her gut
—that if they never captured anything damning, then there would be
no harm; whereas, if she had removed the cameras, she might have
inadvertently tipped her hand to Harper. Taking the cameras down

could easily have piqued Harper's curiosity and caused her to accelerate her investigation of Gia.

Removing the cameras, Gia thought, *would have made me look guilty... even La Nonna agreed.*

Gia's Serbian burner phone zapped her from inside her pocket, and she jumped. She hoped it might be Cameron. As she answered, though, sadness set in, because she wasn't sure if Cameron would ever call her again. Gia touched her stomach, and Cameron's baby flopped inside, the fetus's tail swishing against the inside of Gia's belly.

Maybe the baby would bring him back?

"I am here," *La Nonna* murmured on the other end of the line. "Open the gate for me. And hurry!"

Hiding herself under the covered portion of the courtyard, Gia pressed her back against the wall and edged as quickly as she could to the front gate. When she cracked the heavy entryway open for *La Nonna* to squeeze in, a drone dropped from the sky into the open atrium and hovered, capturing the women on camera.

La Nonna whipped out a canister from her Gucci bag and sprayed in the direction of the camera, covering the lens with black paint. The drone writhed in the air like a dying wasp before slamming against a wall and falling into Gia's pool. The women hustled indoors before another nosy camera flew in.

Once inside, *La Nonna* leaned against the door, huffing, "*Madonna!* What a barbaric invasion of privacy. Such behavior is absolutely prohibited! I will file a petition with the court today to stop this nonsense."

"Come with me," Gia said, pulling *La Nonna* into the master bath and turning on the tub, the shower, and both sinks. For good measure, she also pumped some EDM through the house's speakers. Then, she leaned in and whispered in *La Nonna*'s ear, "It is time to remove these cameras."

"Do not worry, *angioletta,*" *La Nonna* patted Gia's arm as she spoke, "My crew is already on the way. They will sweep everything. For the moment, why do we not sit for an espresso together and be silent? Perhaps put on some more relaxing music?"

Gia nodded. They strode to the kitchen with measured grace, a very convincing effort to appear relaxed. Once there in that inner sanctum, Gia streamed some *Bossa Nova* while she brewed two espressos.

Less than a half an hour later, *La Nonna* opened the front gate for her crew. First they sealed off the courtyard using a thick, opaque tarp that was made from material similar to a ship's sail. The men worked incredibly fast, zipping up and down ladders, hammering and wrapping bungee cords. Next, the crew examined every inch of the house and removed all fifteen of Harper's spy cameras. Once the cameras were gone, Gia retrieved all of her mother's bones from the fireplace and zipped them into a leather duffle. She spared a few very small ones; these she slipped into her pocket.

La Nonna stood over her client. "*Allora,* tell me, did you slit this one's throat as well?"

"Of course not! This is Mamma."

La Nonna's eyes widened as she chomped a biscotti. "How enchanting."

"Put Mamma somewhere safe," Gia pleaded, pressing the duffle bag against *La Nonna.*

The older woman sighed heavily. "Gia," she grimaced as she gripped the handles of the bag. "The Langleys arrived this morning. We must find Cameron before they do, and you must leave Venice tonight."

"Where do you propose that I hide? My jet is still in Greece. And surely the media are watching all my properties."

"I can offer you one solution," *La Nonna* winced.

"Out with it, then." Gia shoved her hand into her pocket and stroked one of her mother's finger bones to soothe her racing heart.

"Sicily."

Gia snorted derisively. "You cannot be serious."

"*Signor* Mosca was quite captivated by you in Athens. He has extended an open invitation to visit his *frutteto di limoni.*"

Crossing her arms in front of her breasts, Gia rolled her eyes and spat, "What a ridiculous man. This idea is absurd."

5

December 20th—Late Afternoon

Harper thumbed through the news feed on her phone. Every major outlet—even the reputable ones—were running stories about The Mermaid and her Mystery Man. Footage of a panicked Cameron exiting Gia's palazzo rolled in a loop, apparently on repeat. Harper's eyes followed him as he bolted down the street that hugged the Cannaregio canal and disappeared into a dark alley.

Where the hell did you go, Cam-Cam? Harper thought for the hundredth time.

Out of habit, she dialed Cam's phone but, as usual, he didn't answer. In her parents' room, on the other side of the suite, the TV blared. They were glued to OTN while Royce texted his army of newsmakers in NYC.

"Harper, get in here!" Royce's voice was thunderous and angry. No matter, she took her time crossing the hotel suite's large living room, stopping to poke at a smoldering log in the fireplace before strolling in to face her father. "I just heard from your producer. Go on, tell your mother what you did."

Bronwyn's icy blue eyes fixed on her daughter. "What did you do?"

"I went on the record," Harper shrugged, as if it had been the most natural thing to do under the circumstances.

"After we specifically told you not to?" Bronwyn hissed through tight lips.

"I held out as long as I could," Harper admitted, "out of respect for you, really. But the story's out there now, Mom. You've seen it. His face is everywhere for God's sake. It's not a secret anymore. We have to face that reality if we want to get control of the narrative."

"Control of the narrative," Royce grunted, tossing his phone onto the other side of the bed, for his wife to pick up. Bronwyn did so as she slipped on her glasses to read the string of texts between Royce and Harper's lead producer.

Bronwyn gasped. "You went to Goldie!"

"Harper," Royce closed his eyes and balled up his fists. "This is way beyond a betrayal... it's a direct violation of your contract with the network."

"A violation of my contract?" Harper snorted. "My brother is missing, his psychopathic *mermaid* girlfriend is across town sitting in a house filled with fucking *bones*... and you're worried about getting scooped? This is a real low for you, huh?"

"Do not speak to your father that way! You're acting like an ungrateful child."

"Ungrateful? I've been by your side not just for these past few weeks, but for years... *years*, Mom. I don't have to take this shit. My coverage of the Nico case brought in record ratings. You are *lucky* that I haven't taken my show elsewhere... *so far.*"

"Sweetheart," Bronwyn rose from her chair and closed the space to stand inches from her daughter, "if you think we won't file an injunction, you are sorely mistaken."

"Sue me then." Harper lifted her manicured thumbs up and shook them in her mother's face. "That's really the smart way to handle things."

Just then, Royce's phone rang, and he fumbled his way across the bed to answer. "Mr. Mayor... I hope you're calling me with good news."

6

May 1994

Pierre reached past the rubber strips that hung from the doorway and felt his way deeper into the darkness. The room vibrated with the latest rave hit by Members of Mayday. This club was huge, and he was lost. When the lights flashed, he realized that everyone was gathering around a pit, and he made his way in that direction, determined to see what was capturing the interest of others.

In the sunken part of the room sat a metal cage, containing two women in latex lingerie. A robust redhead shoved another other woman, a brunette with a pixie cut, onto the floor, forcing her to crawl on her hands and knees. The redhead took bites from an apple and spat them on the floor—and the brunette licked them up, chewed, and swallowed. When the redhead turned toward Pierre, he saw that she was wearing a glass strap-on. His stomach flopped. He'd always been a little scared of lesbians.

He walked on, this time through a corridor that also served as an interactive dungeon. Patrons of the club had booked special appointments in advance. A man screamed as he was flogged against a Saint

Andrew's cross. Farther down was a medical room, where highly unauthorized procedures were underway.

Pierre passed a closed room that was covered in floor-to-ceiling shag carpet. Inside, a group of furries cuddled in a pile. Then, he stumbled upon a rather strange fetish... everyone stood around touching themselves, while watching a woman blow up balloon after balloon until they popped.

Feeling overwhelmed, Pierre wondered where normal people might go to simply make out a little? Having recently split from his wife, he felt all he could really handle tonight was second or third base. He finally fumbled his way back to the bar where he nursed a whiskey and soda, feeling rather disappointed with himself that he wasn't more adventuresome on his first trip to a Berlin sex club. His buddies in Paris would snicker if they saw him now.

A woman in a leather halter top and low-rise silk pants slipped in beside him. The barkeep recognized her, and pulled a bottle from a hiding spot beneath the bar. Kentucky bourbon. Then the bartender poured her a glass and passed her the bottle. She finished topping off the glass herself.

"This is your secret stash?" Pierre attempted to ask, in German.

The woman responded to him in French, "Your German is awful."

He nodded, relieved that she knew his language, and he didn't have to struggle in agony.

"It is very loud here," she said, shouting into his ear. "Would you like to go somewhere more quiet?"

There was nothing he wanted more than that. He nodded again, smiling wide this time.

She motioned to his whiskey soda, "Finish that."

He downed it.

She gave him the bottle of bourbon to hold onto and grabbed his other hand. They snaked through throngs of people and entered a glass elevator in the center of the club's main dance floor. The music level dropped about eighty percent once they got inside. She pressed the button for the fourth floor, and the elevator rose over the crowd. Suddenly, she slammed her hand into the big red STOP button, and the car jerked to a halt. An alarm bell rang out, but she removed a key from her pocket and turned it into a slot in the wall, silencing the alert.

"What if people need to use the lift?" Pierre asked her.

"Then they can fuck off."

He stared at her with wide eyes.

She continued, "My name is Gia. And you?"

"Um... I'm... Florent." Why did he lie? He regretted it the moment the words dropped from his mouth.

Gia took a sip from her glass and narrowed her eyes at him. "Do you like bourbon, Florent?" She slid down to the floor and crossed her legs.

"I think so."

"Would you like to try mine?"

"May I?"

"Come here," she said, patting the floor beside her.

He lowered himself awkwardly.

"Closer, please," she commanded and he schooched. She reached out and ran her hand through his fluffy, light brown hair, grabbing onto a large section of hair near his neck, then yanking his head back.

Stunned, he lost his breath.

She took another swig from her glass and, this time, pushed her lips against his and slowly let the liquid roll into his mouth and onto his tongue. He was instantly hard.

"Very good boy," she whispered.

She brought his head between her breasts. He could smell the mix of leather, sweat, and white florals on her skin. He had obviously stumbled from his boring life into some kind of fever dream. He was forty and fit, thanks to handball three nights a week with his friends, not to mention his daily pull-ups. And he had always had the feeling that his discipline would pay off somehow.

He lifted his head to kiss her, but she snatched it back.

"No," she said, shoving it into her lap. Her long dark hair fell around them like a velvet drape.

7

December 20th—After Dark

Rotating the wheel of the hatch that unlocked her path to freedom, Gia slipped out of the underwater entrance to her house. She flicked her tail as she swam, making sure not to disturb the water. Above her, press boats clanged, and a hundred people talked over one another. She fought the very strong impulse to attack the boats, turn them over, and drown every reporter on board.

Slung across her back was a mesh bag, into which she had sealed up some personal effects in plastic, including her mother's bones. Passing the Lido, Gia swam beyond the Venetian Lagoon and emerged from the water to board a motorboat. Halfway to Croatia, she stopped on a sandbar and waited for her cousin Yiannis to arrive. Sometime in the middle of the night, Gia spotted his glowing eyes drawing ever closer.

"*Koúklaki mou!*" He embraced her. "Can you feel the energy of the sea? The True Alignment is underway. And tomorrow I will participate in the Queen's ceremony."

Tomorrow? Gia thought.

When Gia chose excommunication, she had no idea how expeditiously Queen Zale would get to the business of undoing decades of Gia's hard work.

Yiannis stared into space, to see if he could observe Jupiter and Saturn aligning with the Moon.

"The sea is rising, Cousin. The Gracious Tides will be the end of Man, and the earth will be ours again."

Gia punched him lightly on the arm. "I never imagined you as a religious fanatic, my dear." He snickered, but under his laughter, Gia sensed a steeliness. "Yianni, you cannot leave me."

"Unfortunately I must. You chose your punishment, and now we must all return to the colony."

A sense of desperation swelled in Gia—indeed, the feeling had felt more constant as of late.

"How can I persuade you not to go? The business can survive the loss of the rest of our cousins, but I *need* you. I have not managed operations as you do in more than a decade. Please, stay with me... I will give you half the company. We can start over and hire an entirely new staff."

"*Koúkla mou,*" he sighed. "That is a very tempting offer. I may well run the business again at some point, but that day is not today."

8

"Breaking news." The lower third title on the screen displayed Monica Yung's name and underneath, the channel, LION. "I'm coming to you live from Venice, and I am joined by Harper Langley of OTN."

The camera pulled back slightly to reveal Monica and Harper standing together in front of the oversized wooden doors at Gia's palazzo.

"Harper, I'm told you have come to LION with an exclusive report."

"That's right, Monica. Shortly I will reveal never-before-reported details concerning the woman behind the Mermaid Tape."

"And Harper, I just have to ask, because our audience will want to know... why have you come to LION and not released this story on OTN? After all, the network *is* owned by your family."

"That question is its own story, isn't it, Monica?"

Monica eyed Harper and her lips tightened. "Which is why I'm asking you," she retorted.

"We can cover that at another time," Harper replied, attempting to smile but managing only a smirk.

"All right then, Harper," Monica conceded, "over to you." The camera panned to Harper and zoomed in.

Off camera, Monica fumed.

How dare Goldie foist this airhead on her during her hard-earned prime time hour. Was this going to be a thing from now on, a co-host? Or was Harper there to push out Monica completely? Although her contract wasn't up for two more years, Monica knew the high level of disdain Goldie Stern harbored for aging female anchors.

Harper stared into the lens and spoke to the people of America—and to conservative LION viewers all over the globe. "This story is personal to me. I want that to be clear from the start. I need your help to find my brother, Cameron Langley. He's in trouble. Roll the package, please."

There it was, Harper's spy footage from yesterday inside Gia's house. Cam was in the living room, holding up a long bone. No sound, just grainy night vision footage. Gia entered the room, and her eyes glowed a little. Cameron put the bone down and backed away from her, but she kept pushing toward him. His body was stiff, eyes wide. He held his hands out in front of himself, palms toward Gia, and he nearly tripped several times as he walked backwards—then the tape cut to coverage from the front of the house. Cameron was gone in a flash as countless paparazzi screamed for his attention.

"That must be difficult to watch," Monica said, as the picture returned to the women. "Can you explain to the viewers what transpired?"

"What I can tell you is that I am very concerned for my brother's wellbeing."

"I have lots of questions," Monica continued. "Who is the woman on this footage? Do you have any indication as to whose bones your brother Cameron was holding? Where do you think he is now?"

"I have not personally seen or heard from Cameron in weeks. I fear his life is in danger, and I think, given the chance... that woman... Gia Acquaviva... she'll kill him."

"Wow, Harper," Monica's eyes blinked multiple times, "that's quite an accusation to level at someone on an international news program."

Harper didn't respond to Monica but instead spoke again, straight to camera. "Roll the second package, please."

Now the screen showed security footage from Madrid. Gia walked alongside Nicolás Ángel Fernández. Harper narrated, "If you recall, this footage was released over a month ago, and you can clearly see that the woman on this footage is the very same who was with my brother... Gia Acquaviva. The next clip is quite graphic, so we advise parents with younger children to ask them to leave the room."

In the next tape, Gia straddled Spanish film star, Nicolás Ángel Fernández. Nico wrapped his arms around Gia, but she pushed his arms onto the bed with one hand and violently slapped him in the face with the other. He winced. She kissed his mouth hard and struck his face again.

The camera cut back to Harper. "You can see from this series of clips that Gia Acquaviva was intimately involved with the slain movie star, Nico, whose body was found here in Venice this past September, with a slashed throat. I don't know about you, Monica, but the bone that my brother was holding... I want to know why it was in Gia's fireplace. But more than anything, I want my brother safe and sound... before he turns up just like Nico."

9

December 22nd

S outhwest of Mount Etna laid a thick strip of farmland that ran down the spine of two smaller hills and rolled across the valley, all the way to the Mediterranean. This megaplot and every speck of volcanic dirt on it belonged to *Signor* Quintilio Mosca —or Q, as he was known to the locals. Q had spent the last thirty-five of his fifty-eight years dominating Monopoly until all one hundred and thirty hectares were his. To put that in perspective, his lemon grove, with its rich and verdant landscape, occupied roughly one-half of a square mile, a rather large slice of Sicilian paradise.

"No," Q crooned into a walkie-talkie. "I want it slightly left of where it is now."

Across the valley, on the twin mountain of his estate, Q directed a construction crew. From a large crane dangled a sheet of plexiglass the size of a city block.

"Left!" the architect shouted, after muting the radio on his end. The crane operator strained to hear him. "For Christ's sake," the architect insisted, "I said left! No! The other left." He clicked the button on the walkie-talkie and spoke to his client. "There, sir?"

"That is perfect. The moon will reflect off the water just as I imagined. I love it."

"Very good, sir. We will carry on then."

"Excellent."

In his outdoor kitchen, Q juiced one of his lemons, mixing it with some club soda from the fridge. As he brought the Baccarat tumbler to his face, a tiny bubble burst and splashed onto his aviators. He eased into a chaise lounge covered in orange cashmere and took in the view. Once complete, his aquarium would technically be Europe's largest. He smiled to himself, musing over the thought of all of his dreams coming true.

He picked up his cell phone and dialed *La Nonna*. The line had barely trilled when she answered. "*Signor* Mosca," she said, "how is the sun in the south today?"

"What time is she arriving?"

La Nonna did not respond immediately. On her end of the line, she grimaced, but then plastered on a smile, as if her client could see her, and she tried to inject as much sparkle into her voice as she could muster. "*Signor*, I am afraid Gia has declined your offer."

"Donatella, my darling," his words were smooth, but *La Nonna* braced herself for what came next, "when I request something, do I somehow convey to you that my desires are optional?"

"No, certainly not."

"Hmm."

"I thought... perhaps we would give her the chance to—"

"Where is Gia now? Shall I send my jet?"

"*Signor,* do not worry, I will find her," *La Nonna* insisted, as she tried to maintain her calm.

"Find her? Is she not with you?"

"*Bene, allora...*" She tried to gather her thoughts.

"Donatella, I want her here by Christmas Eve. Am I being plain enough?"

"I understand you, yes. You shall have her by the holiday."

"Good. I would hate for you to *disappear* before Christmas. All those poor grandchildren..."

And with that, he ended the call.

10

December 22nd

Rip Cure looked more like an outpost at a Jimmy Buffet resort than it did the Dakar-based headquarters of a budding surf and skate empire. A young kid grabbed a board and waxed it, before heading toward a sign that read *Plage*. Gia parked her motorcycle between a row of beach huts and approached a group of men sitting around a driftwood table. A tall, thin black fellow stood to greet her.

"Here she is," he grinned, "the world's most famous mermaid."

"I assume you are Prince Moussa?" she inquired, silently critiquing the man who stood before her.

He flung his long locs over one shoulder and raised a hand to the sky, "*Oui. C'est moi.* Come in, come in."

Rushing her inside his surf shop, he proceeded to pour her a cool glass of bissap. He topped it off with a mint leaf, and they took a seat at a bar top table fashioned from a longboard.

"Before we get into it," Moussa started, "I want to let you know... I'm not taking on any more of my mother's little..." he turned his head to the side and squinted at her, "...little *projects*."

"Pardon me?"

"You heard me."

"Queen Awa specifically told me to come to Dakar and find you."

"The Queen commands the colony, not The Prince," Moussa leaned back, flashed a fake smile, then took a sip from his glass.

"Where is your mother?"

"Why do you ask?" Moussa laughed. "Are you unhappy with the service? Would you like to speak with the manager?"

The corners of her mouth slipped down. As a last piece of business with Yiannis, Gia had instructed him to close all of her establishments temporarily. She needed to figure out how to staff up again —and quickly—but with a complex multinational structure, reconfiguring her business without her army of mermaid cousins would be a very complicated undertaking.

Her brain turned over possibilities.

She missed Vittore and wished she'd gone to Santorini to pick him up instead of coming here to Senegal. Vittore always had good ideas. After all, he'd been one of the original architects behind her parents' casinos. The clubs, however, had been Gia's addition to the Acquaviva portfolio.

"What a shame... I came all this way," Gia sighed, placing her empty cup on the table. She reached for her bag to leave. "I suppose I should—"

"Gia," Moussa rolled his eyes, "clearly we're going to host you here. My mother would disown me if I didn't dust the red carpet off for your stay... however brief it may be." He turned his head and yelled over his shoulder, "Oumar! Come in here *mon amour.*"

In walked a barrel-chested man with a short afro fade and a chin beard.

"Gia, this is my husband, Oumar."

"*Enchanté,*" Oumar nodded.

"*Mon amour*, we're ready to head home, can you get the truck ready?" asked Moussa.

* * *

OUMAR UNLOADED the surfboards from the bed of their Nissan pickup. Gia climbed into the back with her Hermès weekender. The men tried to talk Gia into sitting in the front, but she declined. The road was bumpy, and she cradled her belly, because it felt like the tiny mermaid growing inside of her was tumbling in the center of a wave. A motorcycle zipped by them on the crowded roadway carrying a trailer full of onions. They drove by a short hill capped with a statue of a couple holding a baby who pointed to the sky.

Moussa slid the back window open and played tour guide. "African Renaissance Monument," he said, gesturing to the statue.

"It is lovely."

"We all hate it. Colossal waste of money. Typical government bullshit."

After twenty minutes, they arrived at a boat slip. They helped Gia into a motorboat and took off into the Atlantic Ocean. Their destination was an offshore wind farm, in the middle of which was a floating concrete pad housing a service station.

"*Chez nous*," Oumar said, steering his boat toward the middle of the platform. The concrete opened and unfolded, revealing a water-powered boat lift. They sailed in and left the boat in its parking spot. After that, the platform closed itself automatically, concealing the boat. Then, Gia and her new friends boarded a glass elevator and were ferried into the deep sea via its electronic water shaft.

On the way down, Moussa turned to Gia, "We are taking you in from the back entrance. The princes from California are in town. We don't want you running into one another."

"What are they doing here?" Gia probed, quite irritated that he had not relayed this information already.

"It has nothing to do with you, if that's what you're worried about," Moussa chided.

Oumar jumped in, "Moussa and I are part of a task force on oceanic violence, so the princes are here to meet with us about that."

"Oceanic violence?" Gia repeated.

"The barbaric fishing practices that contribute to the climate crisis," Moussa explained. "But we know you're really busy flying around on your jet fixing slot machines and slinging margaritas, so you probably don't know anything about the steps we're taking in the Atargatic community to protect the planet."

"Honestly, Moussa, before a few weeks ago, I had never heard of the Pan-Atargatic Council, so I think your judgment is a bit unfair."

* * *

ONCE THEY ARRIVED at the seafloor, Gia was able to take in the incredible architecture of the Senegalese colony. Moussa had overseen the renovation of the Coral Tower himself, taking inspiration for the underwater skyscraper from the Burj Al Arab, because he loved the whimsy of a colony of mermaids living in a metaphorical ship's sail.

It had taken him thirty years to complete construction, and the result was stunning.

The building was crafted from old-fashioned steel, but the real magic in the design came from the glowing phytoplankton sculptures that twisted through the beams and held the whole structure together. Its architectural beauty far surpassed anything on land.

Along the way to the guest suites, Oumar pointed out special projects that he and Moussa were still completing.

"For Moussa, the work is never done," he laughed. "He calls it 'editing.' I call it what it is... perfectionism."

Moussa shot his husband a nasty look. "And who was it that insisted on crushed pearls in the terrazzo, hmmm?"

Everywhere they walked, Gia was the recipient of stares.

"I imagine everyone has seen the Mermaid Tape?" she whispered.

Oumar let out a deep chuckle. "Darling, I know the colony in Greece is a little provincial, but here in Senegal we do have television."

They rounded the corridor leading to the royal suites.

"And here we are," Moussa led Gia into the finest accommodation in the Tower.

She gazed out the rounded window of her suite and saw what looked to be a cloud made of tiny rainbows.

"Those are sea butterflies," Moussa explained. "It's their migration season."

The tiny creatures' transparent shells were illuminated from within, and when they fluttered by, the kaleidoscope of butterflies reflected color across the suite.

"Shall I ring for tea?" Oumar asked.

"I prefer to rest for a while if that is all right. It was a very long journey to get here."

"Yes, of course," Moussa agreed. "Just please stay in your room tonight. The Californian princes depart in the morning. We certainly would not want you running into each other."

"Will no one from the colony tell them I am here?"

"Absolutely not. We prize discretion above all else. I have let my people know that I expect not one single word to swim its way to Greece. Or any other place for that matter," he added. "You know, Gia... if you've done anything positive for the world of Mermaid, it's that you've united all the colonies against a common enemy."

"I thought Man was the enemy?" Gia snipped.

"And isn't your father human?" Moussa wasted no time delivering another jab.

"He died many years ago."

Gia angled her head as if waiting for another challenge.

"Don't worry yourself too much about it. Queen Awa always roots for the underdog. You can count on Senegalese support."

11

December 23rd

There was a soft knock at the door of Harper's room. After the row with her parents, she'd asked the Concierge of the Hotel Bauman for her own suite on another floor. She glimpsed through the peephole and then let in her guest.

Harper showed Paula Fernández to a loveseat near the fireplace. "Would you like some tea?" Harper asked. "I had room service send me some earlier. It's still hot."

"Wine would be better."

"I have a very nice bottle of red."

"Actually," Paula said, scanning the wet bar, "I will take a Fernet-Branca, and if you do not mind, Harper, please make it a large serving."

Harper passed Paula the whole bottle and an empty tumbler. "Here you go."

"Bless you," Paula replied, twisting off the cap. "Has your brother contacted you?"

Harper blew into her teacup. "Nope."

"How long has it been since you last spoke with him?"

"Seventeen days."

"But you are lucky... you have him on camera just a few days ago. My brother, he—"

"Was missing for fifteen days. I know. I couldn't forget if I wanted to. Paula, how did you handle this? I'm going crazy. Do you know the court blocked our search warrant?"

"On what grounds?"

"Doesn't matter. The mayor let my parents into her place last night anyway, but Gia's gone. I don't know how she was able to sneak out. I've had someone there every single goddamn second since I found out she brought him to Venice."

"How can I help you, Harper? I want to help."

"I think we should do an interview."

Paula winced. Her mother wouldn't like that, especially considering it was her first Christmas without her only son.

"I *must* keep this top of mind," Harper stared down at the fire as she spoke. The flames reflected in her eyes. "I have to dominate the news cycle. If I don't... well, I think being visible is everything. I... I think that might be the only way to smoke Gia out." She shut her eyes for a moment and exhaled deeply. "I miss Cam so much, Paula. There's no way he would disappear and not call me. I just wish I knew that he was okay."

Paula crossed the room and cozied up next to Harper. She removed the teacup from Harper's grasp and placed it on the table, taking Harper's hand in hers. Then Paula focused her warm green eyes on Harper's cold blue gaze, "You will find him soon. I am sure of it."

12

December 23rd

Q kissed his ex-girlfriend's neck as she slept in her bed. Lifting up the sheet to crawl in beside her, he cupped his hand around her breast. She rustled and turned onto her side. He parted her hospital gown in the back and slid inside her. He held her tight around the waist as he thrust himself over and over against her backside. She was awake now, but she kept her eyes closed. How could she struggle anyway? He'd already cut off both of her arms.

When he finished, he switched the light on at her bedside table.

"Look at me," he said.

She turned her head to face him.

"Are you comfortable enough, my darling?"

Her eyes filled with tears. How long would he keep her like this?

"Answer me," his voice was more stern now. "Do you need more morphine?"

She shook her head, no. Mental clarity was the only thing she had left. If he was giving her the choice, she preferred that he not take that from her as well. He gently pushed her curls away from her cheeks and stroked her face. He tiptoed his fingers across what remained of her lips. He'd burned her mouth nearly closed with a hot iron months ago. There was just enough space on one side for a feeding tube.

He slid to the edge of the bed and took her right foot into his hands, massaging it. "It is almost Christmas. Do you know what I am giving myself as a gift?" He smiled softly and patted her feet. "These."

He stood and cracked the door. A woman in a uniform entered the room. She carried with her a pail filled with nail polishes and pedicure equipment. Q reached into the bucket and pulled out an orangey-red shade. "This color is very nice." He tossed the small bottle on the bed.

Sighing with deep satisfaction, he left the room.

Down the hall, in a locked cell, a man called out desperately for help. Q strolled over and slid open a tiny window.

"May I help you with something?" Q asked, in English.

On the other side of the steel bars, Cameron looked back at his captor in terror.

13

December 23rd

Gia slipped into a pair of shorts, and discovered that the top button wouldn't close. Definitely a first for her. Compromising, she opted to fold the waistband down and tie her silk shirt so that it hung over the zipper. She really wasn't in the mood to discuss her pregnancy and hoped no one would notice. Her night in the Senegalese colony had been very pleasant, and she had slept well.

Oumar arrived at Gia's suite to escort her to the Tower's central dining room, which was spacious and grand, for a light brunch. The space itself reminded her of the ballroom in her Macau casino. In fact, with the warm glow all around, it offered her the same tingling sensation that she got when she first walked into her parents' casino in Venice—the feeling that anything is possible.

Moussa's table was next to a large, sparkling fountain. He dipped a champagne flute under the mouth of one of the fountain's many glass seahorses, and then passed the bevvy to Gia.

"Drink up, Gia. It's totally dry in Dakar, so you should enjoy the libations down here."

"No, thank you." She took her place across the table from Moussa. "None for me."

"Oh," he said, his eyes narrowing a bit, "I would have thought all that murdering made you thirsty."

"Pardon me?"

"Never you mind!" He tipped his glass to his husband. "*A nous, mon amour.*"

Oumar kissed Moussa on the cheek and swallowed a gulp of bubbly.

"Have the Californian princes left?" Gia inquired.

"Would you be out of your room if they had not?" Moussa retorted. "Shall we get on with it, then?" he asked, refilling his glass. "Why exactly have you come to Senegal?"

"Are you sure you would not prefer to wait until your mother returns to discuss business?"

"Really?" Moussa turned his head down and bore his deep brown eyes into Gia. "Do you think a grown merman needs his *mother* around to make decisions for him?"

Gia was not sure what to say. Men always bent to her will. Therefore, she found Moussa rather tedious.

"My apologies, Prince Moussa. You are absolutely correct. I have not treated you with the respect that befits a man of your stature."

Moussa giggled to himself and Oumar poked him between the ribs. "My husband is being stubborn, Gia."

"As is his right," she replied.

"Please do not encourage him," Oumar continued. "If he gets any worse, we might have to ship him off to live with the mermaids in the Arctic Circle!"

"Ha!" Moussa lightly slapped his husband's hand. "My tail would fall off! Would you like that? A husband with no tail? I think not!"

Oumar tossed his hands up in feigned exasperation as Moussa returned his attention back to the matter at hand.

"Cards on the table, Gia. What is it that you want?"

"I loved your little surf shop, Moussa. I read online that you are hoping to expand your line into Asia."

"What concern is that of yours?" Moussa's irritation was clear.

"I know how expensive expansion into APAC can be... that is all."

"And what in the Gracious Tides' name makes you think I would need your money?

"I do not *think* you need my money. On the contrary, I *know* you need it."

Moussa whispered to Oumar, "She has some nerve."

"Is that not why your mother is in Hong Kong now? Negotiating for investment capital?"

Moussa turned his nose up and took another sip from his glass.

"I am well aware that the colony is already highly leveraged." She waved an arm around the room. "Beautiful buildings cost money, Moussa."

"Is this your sales pitch to me? Calling me broke? Give me one reason I should not have Oumar drop you off at the beach right now and let you drive off on your sad little motorbike."

"*Bene...* because I would like to offer you a partnership."

"A partnership in *what*?"

"My full portfolio. Two casinos in Europe, five clubs. Two clubs in South America. A beautiful beach club in Sydney, and a gorgeous little casino in Macau that I know you will love."

Moussa furrowed his brow, trying to work out Gia's angle. "I'm confused."

"It is the perfect opportunity for each of us. You need capital, and I need staff. I also know that your colony... unlike mine in Greece... is quite reliant on imports. Since you finished construction on the Tower, many of your residents have been... how shall I phrase this? Underemployed."

Moussa turned to his husband and began chattering away in French.

"What do you think, Prince Moussa?" Gia asked, drawing his attention away from his husband and back to her.

"I think that this conversation is over," he snapped.

"But we have only begun negotiating," Gia insisted.

"This is your idea of doing business? I invite you into my home, into my mother's queendom and you insult me, a royal? I think not. Your stay is over. It was lovely having you visit Dakar. Swim on home, little mermaid. *Adieu.* Our business is concluded."

"Prince Moussa, I *sincerely* apologize... you are right... I have not been myself." She paused and leveled her gaze. "It must be the hormones from the baby."

"You're pregnant?" he asked, his eyes wide.

She nodded.

"That is wonderful," Oumar smiled. "Blessings to you and your child. You have given Moussa a lot to think about, Gia. Perhaps, for now, it is best if you go. I cannot speak for Moussa, and the decision about the partnership is his to make. However, the Queen has made it clear that Senegal will stand behind you, and so we must. Perhaps we can set a call to speak about this in the new year?"

14

December 24th

Q had the construction teams working around the clock. Everyone promised him that the aquarium would be finished by the new year. *It damn well better be*, he thought.

He had already lined up every truck in Italy to start delivering tanks of water on the first of January. It would take three weeks to dump twelve million liters into his gigantic glass box and he wanted it done as soon as possible.

At that moment, across the orchard, a crew worked inside the aquarium building a small castle.

But where was his mermaid?

La Nonna had not answered his calls, which clearly meant that she was not in possession of Gia, the centerpiece of all of his grand designs.

As the hours passed, his annoyance transitioned into rage. This certainly was not what he had planned for Christmas. He ducked downstairs to check in on his ex-girlfriend, hoping that would cheer him up. Unfortunately, there was bad news on that front as well.

"I am very sorry, *Signor* Mosca," the surgeon said, head lowered, "she did not survive."

Q examined the operating table. There laid his lover, with her Venus di Milo arms and only one foot, which balanced precariously in a pool of thick blood and juicy fibers.

"She hemorrhaged," the doctor explained, "and we were not able to stem the loss."

"How could you let this happen?" Q demanded, cradling his hand under her head and lifting it toward him.

"This was always a risk, as I explained, *Signor* Mosca. She has been bedridden for so long without solid food. Her body..." the man had to steady himself on the edge of the table. He never imagined that after graduating at the top of his class that he would ever be involved with something as depraved and macabre as this. "Sir, her body had deteriorated since the last procedure."

"Did you save the other foot at least?"

"Yes, I have sent it to be preserved, as you requested."

"Fine. Fine. Then take her body to the crematory."

The doctor signaled for the nursing staff to bring the gurney. They were about to load her lifeless corpse when Q suddenly became enraged and lunged toward the body, taking into his hands a large section of the woman's hair, trying to rip it all out.

The doctor sprinted over with a pair of scissors, as if doing further damage to the body was unthinkable, especially after all that had already occured. "Please, take these."

Q grasped her mane in his hand and sawed until he held her curly ponytail between his knuckles. He took in the gruesome sight before him and turned away. "She looks disgusting. Get her out of my sight."

He pressed the intercom and summoned several of his men downstairs, lining up about five of them in the hallway.

"I am very unhappy. Very displeased. This is not a good day, and nothing is going to plan." Q sulked as he led them down the corridor and unlocked Cameron's cell. "Take him." Two of the larger men entered and grabbed Cameron from where he cowered on the dirt floor.

Cameron eyed the handful of dark hair Q was holding and deduced correctly that it came from the head of the woman whom he'd heard moaning every night since his arrival in this deathtrap.

"Please," he begged, "I have money, my family has money. My parents, they own—"

"I know everything about you. I do not need your money, and I do not need you. Not a moment longer. I need something else." Q cupped his hands around his lips and yelled down the hall. "*Dottore!* Bring a sedative!"

Cameron twisted and fought, but he wasn't strong enough to break away. When the doctor poked him with the syringe, everything around him became twilight brown for a second, and his body tingled. After that, the lights went out.

"Slit his throat," Q ordered, "and drop him in the Rio di Cannaregio near Gia's place."

15

July 1994

Pierre's real estate broker thought of himself as a cheeky person. So, for a lark, he had threaded a silver replica of the Eiffel Tower onto Pierre's new keychain. The keys jingled as Pierre swung open the ornate door of his new crashpad.

His dalliance with Gia in Berlin had invigorated him, and he now felt much more comfortable taking on lovers. So much so that he had reached the point where it was a necessity to arrange a place to take all the women as he really didn't want his son walking in on him at home. Despite the fact that the divorce was finished and Pierre was on good terms with his ex—*very* good terms, especially after a few recent visits—he sensed that his son was still feeling sensitive about the whole thing.

Pierre purchased this new apartment with some of the funds associated with the pending acquisition of his SMS technology company.

Oh, if his father could see him now.

His old man had balked when Pierre announced his intention to study computer science at university. *Monsieur* Bisset always assumed that his son would take over operations of the family biscuit company in Brittany. When Pierre did not ascend to the cookie throne, the job fell to his younger sister. No matter, all that business was ancient history. He was now in possession of a panty-dropping, classic Paris apartment, freshly renovated with an impressive two-story terrace garden that featured a hot tub with a view of the Eiffel Tower.

However, if Pierre had been really honest with himself, he would have realized that the driving factor in his real estate purchase was competition.

Deep down, he wanted to impress Gia.

He had flown back to Berlin twice to see her after their first tryst. She had impressed him as she was busy running the club and stuffing away enough dough to make an all-cash offer on a trendy little beach bar located on the Amalfi Coast.

Gia was a seriously intimidating person and Pierre had never met such a single-minded, career-focused woman in his life. She didn't even make time for friendships. It was all-systems-go, all of the time with her.

The truth, at the bottom of it, was that Pierre felt certain that Gia was way out of his league.

Miraculously, he had finally convinced her to sneak away to Paris to meet him. Surely a sunset cocktail in his new rooftop hot tub off of the swanky Avenue George V would go a long way toward evening their odds?

Presently, there was absolutely no furniture in his apartment except for a bed. Pierre stuffed a bottle of Veuve into the fridge and then unsealed a package of Frette sheets. He'd read somewhere that Frette was the *crème de la crème*, and for the ungodly price he paid for one set of bed linens, he really hoped they lived up to the hype.

Just before sunset, Gia pressed the buzzer down on the street entrance as planned. Pierre retrieved her and, together, they rode the rickety antique brass elevator up to the top floor. If Gia was impressed, she didn't let on, to Pierre's dismay. But he grinned to mask his deflation and poured champagne into the apartment's only two glasses. He went in for a kiss, and she turned her head, so his lips landed near her ear.

"What do you think?" he asked, showing her around the place.

"It is very French," she replied flatly, as she stepped out onto the terrace.

He took her hand and led her up the spiral steps to the hot tub. "Shall we get in?"

"Why not?" Gia shrugged, slipped off her crushed velvet babydoll dress, and stood in front of him, wearing only a lacy thong. No matter how many women he bedded, not one compared to Gia.

"May I?" he asked, tracing the top of her panties. She placed both of his hands on her hips and helped him tug them off. Then she bent over the edge of the hottub, and dipped her hand into the water. He moved her hair to the side and kissed her from her shoulders, down her spine and then lower, between her cheeks. He spread her legs and let his tongue explore every place between her thighs.

That afternoon, he discovered how much she enjoyed anal.

She sat on his lap in the water, and he thrust all of himself deep inside of her. After he came, she straddled one of the hot tub jets and pleasured herself as he watched. He could not have been more entranced by her performance.

They floated in the water for hours, until their fingers pruned and Paris lit itself from the inside out.

"How many people do you think are making love right now?" Gia asked, her voice soft and tender.

"Maybe thousands," Pierre whispered, feeling content, "but I am sure that no one is as happy as I am at the moment."

He wanted so much to tell her that he had fallen in love with her. The words were on his lips, but just as quickly as she had opened herself up to him, she now closed herself off again. He watched as she rose and stepped out of the jacuzzi to dry her body with a towel. Afterward, she strode off without uttering a single word to him. How could she turn so cold so quickly? He felt crushed by her ability to flip the switch on and off like that. He sat in the bubbly water naked and alone, feeling as though his chest might collapse in on him.

16

Christmas Day

The staff at the Venice morgue had tried to liven up their workplace for the holiday, and a sad little bit of tinsel draped from the ceiling while a skeleton that stood in the corner donned a Santa cap. Nearby, Cameron's lifeless body rested on a metal table, cold and unadorned.

Harper gazed down at her big brother and tugged the sheet back to his waist, exposing the slash in his neck. Her parents waited in the hallway for her. Neither had the fortitude to speak to the coroner, so Harper was forced to navigate this unthinkable conversation alone. Blistering resentment coursed through her veins.

"What time was he found yesterday?" she asked.

"*Signorina* Langley, I am so very sorry for your loss," the coroner responded, looking up from a file.

"Time of death?" Harper insisted, impatience creeping into her voice.

The man grimaced, as he took in her strange countenance. He had observed countless faces of the loved ones who had lost someone. He knew all about what shock did to a person. That wasn't what he witnessed in Harper, though. Her energy lacked something indescribable—was it humanity, empathy, connection? The thought chilled him.

"He was found shortly after twenty-one-hundred hours last night... however, I must tell you that in my investigation, I encountered some abnormalities."

"Abnormalities?" she spat.

"No signs of struggle. And it appears that he was transported."

"From where?"

"The condition of his body indicates that he—" the coroner stopped himself from using sterile medical language, and instead switched to a more personal way of communicating about someone's dead brother. It was Christmas, after all. "He passed away several hours before."

"How many hours? Is it possible to tell?"

"I am waiting on lab results that will provide more precise information. However, there is also the matter of the toxicology report."

"What about it?" The edge in Harper's voice was more than clear now.

"Unfortunately, those tests are processed in another lab. And that lab is closed for the holidays."

"So, they should open tomorrow, right? It will be December twenty-sixth."

He frowned. "No, it is closed until eleventh January."

"Are you *fucking* kidding me?" Harper bit her lip to keep herself from picking up the nearest object and throwing it. "I want those results the second they are available. And if they can be rushed, I *need* you to rush them."

"I understand, and I will do my best."

"Good."

"One last matter, *Signorina* Langley... do you need our office to help with the transportation of the body to the United States?"

She suddenly looked at the coroner blankly. Harper hadn't thought of that. Taking a dead body back to the States meant a funeral. There was no way she was planning a funeral right now. Not until after she could have Gia arrested.

"Cremate him," she answered, exhibiting no hesitation in her decision making, and showing no consideration of what her parents might want. She pulled the sheet up and over her brother's head. "It will be easier to take him home that way."

17

Christmas Day

La Nonna watched as her grandchildren played in the garden. This year's holiday was practically the same as all of the others—big meals at her daughter's vacation home on Lake Como, a spin in the family boat on Christmas Eve, and lots of presents. Except this Christmas, which had always been her favorite time of the year, *La Nonna* was riddled with untamed anxiety and found herself peeking past the hedges, straining her eyes to discern even the slightest out-of-place motion.

For the first time ever, she had disappointed Q. Were his men on the way to kidnap her now?

She had always wondered whether she and her top client would come to a precarious juncture in their relationship. As his fixer, she fully understood the monstrous acts that he was capable of perpetrating. Perhaps it was naivety or overconfidence, but prior to this, *La Nonna* had considered herself insulated from his ire.

Admittedly, she had made a major miscalculation in failing to recognize the severity of his growing obsession with Gia. Of course, having her life threatened was always an occupational hazard—but up until now it had been a hypothetical one.

Even if she was able to wrangle Gia and deliver her, what would happen the next time she disappointed Q? The seed of a thought began that day: Was it possible to check *Signor* Mosca's power somehow? To ever so slightly destabilize him?

Once again, out of habit this time really, *La Nonna* dialed Gia's phone. *La Nonna* had already fanned out her network, checking every one of Gia's casinos and clubs, as well as all of her known residences, but Gia wasn't anywhere they searched. Recognizing the obvious, *La Nonna* conceded that the escaped mermaid could very well be at the bottom of the sea.

Yet again, as *La Nonna*'s call burst through the airwaves from Italy to some unknown place, there was no answer on the other end of the line. *La Nonna* threw her head back and looked up to the heavens in exasperation.

Then, a flash of inspiration struck: Gia had not mentioned Vittore when *La Nonna* was helping her fend off the horde of news reporters at Gia's palazzo.

Had *La Nonna* overlooked the very salient fact that Vittore never made it back to Italy? And if that were the case... well, the only logical conclusion was that he must still be in Greece. *La Nonna* doubted very much that he was hiding in some underground cavern. No, in her gut, she knew that Vittore was somewhere on land, more specifically, that he was somewhere on the island of Santorini, where Gia's jet was still parked.

She felt practically jubilant as she reached for her phone.

18

Christmas Day

Paris was misty and cold. Gia pulled the collar of her coat up around her neck, and tucked in the long blonde strands of her wig. She would have asked the taxi driver to close the window, but she thought it better if she spoke as little as possible. Tipping her fur cap lower on her head until it met her large sunglasses, she folded into herself.

Out the window, she glimpsed her club, La Perle Noire. Several bored reporters stood outside the bolted front door, watching a woman wash the windows. Closed doors meant mounting costs and no money coming in, and that realization bred anxiety.

She hoped Moussa would come through for her with reinforcements—and soon.

Gia slid deeper into the backseat to avoid any stray cameras. Finally, the driver turned off Avenue George V and onto a little street behind the Four Seasons. Thank God she'd had the foresight all those years ago to keep Pierre's place and put it in the name of an offshore trust.

However, just to be cautious, she asked the driver to stop in front of a different building, paid for the cab in cash, and waited for him to drive away. Once he was gone, she took her bag and rushed inside the building before anyone noticed her.

Dust tornados spiraled as she lifted a sheet off the Roche Bobois sectional. She tossed her bag to one side and fell backward into the cushions. The muscles around her waist twinged.

Gia had no idea if this cramping was normal or not.

She really should have asked the doctor back in Greece more about what to expect while she was expecting, but there was too much on her mind at the time. She had been quite distracted by Cameron's boy-like wonder at the colony and his enthusiasm about his first child.

As she thought of Cameron, her chest tightened. She really missed him. Her eyebrows scrunched up on their own, and somewhere in the depths of her mind, a thought crystalized: Maybe she could win him back. It was worth a try.

He is probably in New York now celebrating with his family, she thought.

She remembered the scene at Thanksgiving, all the decorations... the pie... Harper's angry outburst.

Reaching into her bag, Gia withdrew from it the engraved silver rattle from Bronwyn.

Why had she dragged that damn thing halfway around the world with her?

She placed it on the coffee table and took out her mother's tiny bones, nestling them into the curve of the rattle. Her shoulders slumped, and her head lowered. She stayed in that prone position for a long time, eyeing the bones and the noisy hunk of silver from Tiffany.

This was all she had left from her baby's two grandmothers.

Gia felt uncomfortably restless. She wasn't used to sadness—she never stayed still long enough to feel it. How different things had become. She hated feeling downtrodden, but even more than that, she loathed this feeling of being trapped.

In the distance, lights shimmered on the Eiffel Tower. She rose and lingered near the doors to the terrace, but dared not go outside on the off chance that she'd be spotted by a neighbor. As the laser at the top of the tower scoured the night sky, Gia's mind buzzed not only about Cameron, but also about Pierre.

Everyone who loves me gets hurt.

"*Buon Natale,*" Gia whispered, rubbing her belly. "Baby, we will figure out everything, I promise." She allowed herself one moment to think about next Christmas: She imagined Cam and Vittore in her palazzo both fussing over the baby, as they indulged in big bowls of pasta next to the fire. It was a beautiful fantasy, and it calmed her immensely. She took the bones and rattle into her hand and pattered off to bed.

19

December 26th

When Q's plane touched down at Thira airport, the guys in the control tower marveled over the sight. The men could not get over how much the aircraft looked like a fighter jet.

As instructed, they had temporarily disconnected the power and purposely failed to follow the backup protocols. There would be no record whatsoever of this beautiful, odd little plane landing in Santorini.

And based on the amount of cash that had been promised to them for concealing the arrival and departure of this matte black jet, it was safe to assume that whomever was inside that plane was a bigwig.

The airstairs lowered and a short grey-haired woman emerged. She made her way up the elevator and into the control room. *La Nonna* handed each of the men a large stack of euros and was gone as quickly as she'd come.

A black Mercedes SUV zipped onto the tarmac, and two rough-looking men climbed into the car, flanking *La Nonna* on either side.

Vittore had no idea what was coming for him.

* * *

A FRAPPÉ PASSED under Vittore's nose, its aroma tickled his nostrils.

"No, please," Vittore begged. "Not this again." He covered his head with the pillow from Stavros's bed.

"Just try it, for me. You will love it."

Vittore made a sour face and curled his lips around the paper straw. After one tiny sip, he screamed, "Disgusting! I knew it!"

Stavros belted out a rich laugh and poured Vittore an espresso instead. As he passed it to him he said, "Here, for my young Italian lover, my special brew."

"Young?" Vittore blew air through his lips. "Ha! I have not been young in forty years."

"Now, now," Stavros said, sitting at the end of the bed in his big suite, "I am at least twice your age... I cannot bear to tell you the real number. So, truly, to me, you are practically a teenager."

They held hands and turned their heads to the window, glancing past the plunge pool, to take in the one hundred eighty degree view of the blue sea.

Vittore had not been this happy since... certainly not since Luca died, but maybe... maybe he had never been as happy as he was these past few days with Stavros. He tugged on his lover's beard.

"How about some breakfast?" Stavros winked.

Just as Vittore opened his mouth to reply, there was a knock at the door. One of Stavros's sons stood on the other side.

"*Bampa*," the wide-chested man said in Greek, "there is a woman here for Vittore."

"Is it Gia?" Stavros called.

"No, she said her name is Donatella."

"Hmm, strange." He spoke in Italian over his shoulder to Vittore, "A Donatella is in reception for you."

"Donatella?" Vittore racked his brain but came up empty. He

scrambled to make himself decent and shuffled down the hallway behind Stavros.

On the other side of the marble reception desk stood *La Nonna*.

"Father in the Sky!" Vittore said. "What in all the saints' names are you doing here?"

La Nonna strode across the room and took his hand in hers. "Gia sent me."

He felt himself stumble backward, and Stavros rushed to steady him.

"Come, Vittore," Stavros directed, "sit please."

La Nonna eased into a chair next to him. "Gia asked me to bring you back to Italy."

"Why is she not here herself?"

La Nonna lowered her voice to a whisper. "Does it seem like a good time for a mermaid to be flying around, picking up some old man from the Greek Islands, while the world media searches for her? I do not think so."

"But, where is she?"

"She is safe, relax now. *Bene, allora*, shall we pack a bag and go?"

"This instant?"

La Nonna laughed. "Unless you have..." her voice trailed off and then picked back up again with great drama, "...*something better to do?*" Her eyes grazed around the room and then landed on Stavros. She raised her eyebrows at him several times, suggestively.

"I shall come with you," Stavros said to Vittore.

"Oh, no, absolutely not," *La Nonna* interjected. "That is not advisable at the moment. Gia quite specifically instructed me that Vittore should come alone."

"I see." Vittore cast his eyes to the floor. He was sure he would find his heart down there somewhere as well, waiting to be stamped on. Of course he wanted to see Gia, but this time with Stavros had been magical. He was afraid to leave, lest the spell be broken.

Stavros saw how downtrodden Vittore looked, and he reached down and lifted Vittore's chin.

"Cheer up, young one," Stavros said. "Now that I have found you again, I do not intend on letting you go so easily." He brushed aside what little hair Vittore had left on his scalp and kissed the top of his head.

Vittore sighed. "I have indeed missed my *sirenetta*." He gazed into Stavros's eyes, "I suppose it is back to reality for us, then."

"Hardly," Stavros whispered. "I do not know about you, young man, but I am still walking in the clouds."

20

October 1994

A bottle of vintage Dom Pérignon clinked, nestling against the champagne bucket as the ice shifted. On a small stage, pink lasers illuminated the naked bodies of a row of dancers, all of whom wore identical white stilettos.

Gia took in the scene from the owner's booth.

She was a part of the action and apart from it, which, coincidentally, was her favorite way to move through the world. With deep red lips and dark hair, Gia looked like the leading lady in a spy film.

Pierre rested his hot palm on her knee, wondering if he should slide his hand under the skirt of her black leather halter dress. The bare-breasted performers interested Pierre very little. After all, he already had the biggest prize—the beautiful woman sitting beside him, who had just purchased this club. He was there as her guest, a rather thrilling privilege.

At intermission, the glowing red lamps on the cabaret tables lit the room like fifty psychedelic strawberries.

"*Mesdames et Messieurs*," the handsome emcee smiled as he addressed the patrons, "while we wait for the ladies to slip into something a little more comfortable, please allow me to perform for you a most curious feat of magic. You see, my mother was a witch, and she educated me in the dark arts."

He reached into the coat pocket of his tuxedo jacket and revealed a deck of cards as he fluidly swanned his arm up and tipped off his top-hat. With the other hand, he arched the cards in his fingers, and they flew, one by one, into his hat. When every last card landed inside, he rotated the hat three times to the right, thumped its hard edge and turned the hat upside down.

Not one card fell.

He angled the hat back on top of his black hair and glided over to a nearby table, where he got down on one knee.

"*Madame,*" he said to a bewildered redhead, "would you be so kind as to examine my hat?" The emcee lowered his head, and she nervously removed the top-hat. "Turn it over, please." She followed his command. "Look inside! What do you see?"

"It's empty," she replied, her voice blank with a hint of confusion.

"I see. How strange. Where have the cards gone? I seem to have misplaced them. *Messieurs,* would you please reach into your pockets and show the contents to us?"

Several men pulled out their wallets, but the redhead's husband was shocked to discover that the entire stack of cards was stashed in his front pocket.

"They're here!" The husband called out. "How did you do that?" He hadn't felt a thing.

The emcee winked. "Ah! It is just a little pirate magic... that is all." The crowd howled with thunderous applause, and the band played as the emcee disappeared behind the stage curtain.

Pierre leaned in, kissing Gia on the neck. "Congratulations," he whispered. "How fortunate for me that your Amalfi deal fell through. Perhaps I will have the pleasure of hosting you more often here in Paris."

"Perhaps." Gia's cheeks dimpled as she took a sip of bubbly.

A voice interrupted their flirtation. "Fancy seeing you here, *Signo-*

rina Acquaviva." The emcee titled his hat toward Gia at the same moment that Pierre felt his chest flash hot.

Gia grabbed the man's hand and pulled him onto the seat next to her, "*Astéri mou!*" Once snuggled in, he planted a kiss on Gia's lips. Pierre felt all the air leave his lungs as he watched this exchange with strained eyes.

"Thank you very much for this job," the emcee said, holding Gia's gaze.

"Dimitri, I am so pleased you accepted. Who would imagine that you are not only a star but also a shrewd business manager as well?"

"Excuse me," Pierre leaned in. "Do you know one another?"

Gia and Dimitri wrinkled their noses at each other. "Dimitri is an old family friend," Gia replied.

Dimitri turned his brown eyes toward Pierre. "Forgive me," he bowed his head in a gesture of respect, "I do not mean to intrude on your private time."

"It is no bother," Pierre lied. "Glass of champagne?"

"I would love nothing more," Dimitri said, lifting the corner of his mouth into a lopsided smile. Something about Dimitri's earnest face disarmed Pierre.

"Dimitri, this is my..." Gia's eyes locked with Pierre's. "My boyfriend, Pierre Bisset."

Boyfriend?! Pierre's heart leapt at the thought and he accidentally over-served Dimitri. A bit of excess champagne dripped onto Dimitri's lap. "My apologies!" Pierre ripped the cloth from the champagne bottle and dabbed at the liquid that was now pooling on the front of Dimitri's pants.

Dimitri rested his fingertips on the back of Pierre's hand. "I do not mind getting a little wet," Dimitri said with a smirk.

"Incorrigible," Gia fussed.

Pierre raised his flute to Gia. "To my *girlfriend*, Gia, you stun me with your beauty and your intelligence."

"Here, here," Dimitri offered up his own toast in reply. "*Signorina* Acquaviva is lucky in business *and* in love." The three glasses clinked.

"Are you at the Four Seasons?" Dimitri asked Gia.

"No," Gia scooted a little closer to Pierre. "Pierre has the most charming apartment in Paris, and it happens to be just around the corner."

"Is that so?" Dimitri squared his shoulders against the banquette, cozying up to the couple. But then, in the background, the drummer began whacking on the snare and the volume of the band swelled. Dimitri frowned. "The stage is calling for me... what a shame." He shot up and breezed backstage.

When the curtains lifted, a giant teddy bear occupied the stage. The bear's shoulders were slumped, and he looked forlorn. The floor parted and an oversized rhinestone-encrusted baby crib rose from the underbelly of the stage. Balancing on the crib's sparkling rail was a woman wearing a white bow the size of her head and an empire-waist negligée.

Dimitri entered from stage left, holding a saxophone. He spread his lips and took the mouthpiece in. After a few smooth bars, the bass guitar joined in, and the woman began singing "My Heart Belongs to Daddy." As she chirped, she wiggled her way down the bars of the crib and over to the teddy bear.

At the end of the first verse, she leaned over the stuffed animal's leg, and Dimitri slipped off her lacy bloomers. Underneath was another pair of panties with a big pink heart on the center. Below that pair another.

In the final verse, she climbed up the bear to its shoulder, and crouched on her hands and knees. She circled her hips as she sang the lyrics. At the end of the song, she shimmied out of the final pair of panties and wrapped her legs around the teddy bear's neck, dropping herself so that she was hanging upside down, directly over the bear's stitched mouth. Dimitri tossed his sax to the band and caught the singer as she released her grip and fell from the bear into his arms. They danced together, and then he wrapped her body over the bear and gave her a good spanking.

Gia darted her gleaming eyes over to Pierre and whispered, "This place is going to make a killing."

21

December 26th

The harsh trill of Gia's burner phone woke her from a nap. She answered and was surprised to discover that while she had expected *La Nonna* on the line, it was someone else entirely.

"Gia?"

"Vittore?" she exclaimed, now fully awake. "Is that you? Wait, why are you with *La Nonna*? Is she in Greece? What is going on?" Every warning flag was raised in Gia's mind as she struggled to understand what was happening.

"She told me you wanted me to come to Sicily..." the old man said, voice rife with confusion. Then, there was a muffled scratching sound and she couldn't hear Vittore anymore.

"Vittore??" she yelled into the phone.

"*Signorina* Acquaviva," Q's voice on the line was as light as cotton candy, "I have to say, I was quite wounded when you did not accept my invitation to spend Christmas together. At least we still have New Year's Eve."

Gia furrowed her brow even as her stomach lurched. "Who is this? What is happening?"

"You wound me, Gia. This is Quintilio Mosca. I thought you would remember me from our meeting in Athens. Since you did not accept my invitation to come voluntarily, our mutual friend Donatella had the marvelous idea to bring your friend Vittore for a stay in Sicily. She thought perhaps that might motivate you to take the trip as well. Where are you?"

Suddenly, Vittore screamed in the background.

"Do not come here, *tesoro mio*! I have a bad feeling about this man!"

"Take him downstairs to the vacant room," Q ordered. "*Bella sirena*, I hope that you will not keep me waiting any longer. One question... how old is Vittore?"

Bile rose in Gia's throat, but she swallowed hard and spat her next words.

"Do not do anything to harm him—or I swear I will kill you."

"Sometimes unexpected things happen to old men," Q said simply, "and they just drop, you know? Now, tell me where you are, and I will come and get you. As long as you are with me, you will be shielded from the media and Vittore will be safe. You have my word."

Gia tried to think through her options but felt dazed as she realized she only had one choice.

"Pick me up at Le Bourjet airport tomorrow at noon."

"Oh, I *do* love Paris," Q mused. "Hmm... instead of meeting me at the airport, come to the Eiffel Tower. I will arrange a private lunch at Jules Verne before we fly to Sicily."

"Sounds grand. *Allora, ci vediamo domani.*"

"Yes," Q laughed. "Tomorrow is another day."

She hung up and immediately dialed Great Uncle Stavros in Santorini. He answered right away. Before he could even say a word, she screamed into the phone, "Vittore is in trouble!"

"What? No! Gia? Where are you? Where is Vittore?"

"He is in Sicily. *La Nonna* gave him over to some insane mafioso. The man, Quintilio Mosca... he threatened me."

"I will take the first flight!" Uncle Stavros said, his voice shaking with rage and worry.

"No. I will go to Sicily first and then... if I am able to... I will send word for you by way of my lawyer, *La Nonna*. I do not know what to expect from this man, but he is dangerous. We have to approach the situation with caution. I will not allow Vittore to get hurt. Also, reach out to Queen Awa in Senegal. She will most certainly help us."

Uncle Stavros breathed fast and heavy on the other end of the line. "I cannot lose Vittore, Gia. Do you understand? I cannot."

"Neither can I," Gia said, choking back tears.

22

December 27th

"Harper! How could you do this to me?" Bronwyn wailed. "I'll never see my son again!" She wept into Royce's arms. "My only son!"

In her cold heart, Harper was crying, too, but no one could see. Her tears ripped through her insides like acid rain. Everything hurt. She felt raw.

"Mother," she pleaded, "I'm so sorry. I made a split-second decision... you and Daddy weren't in there with me. You didn't see Cam-Cam, Mom. It's better this way. I know it is."

"Good God, Harper!" Bronwyn broke free of Royce's embrace and screamed at her daughter. "They *burned* his body. Burned him! We can't give him a Christian burial. No one blessed his body! My son... my son..." she sobbed. "He was alone, and he was burned up to nothing, all by himself. I can't stand it. I can't—" Bronwyn lost control of herself and collapsed onto the bed, convulsing with sorrow.

Royce's chin began to tremble. "It's not right what you've done, Harpie." He twisted his neck, turning his head away from Harper, as if looking at her was too much of a betrayal. "You had no right. You should have asked us. You should have." He wandered around the room in a daze, mumbling to himself. "Oh, God. I've made her like this. It was me. This is my fault." He leaned his head on the wall of the hotel suite, trying to hold himself up, to support himself in his grief.

Harper's stomach twisted around itself, and she struggled to catch her breath. She felt panic setting in and her vision became blurry and tunneled as she backed away from her parents. "I'll fix it," she muttered.

Bronwyn couldn't hear anything. Her brain roared with despair. She felt she might die, and, in fact, she wanted to.

Royce had heard his daughter, though. "How on earth can you say that? There's nothing you can do. Nothing at all. You can't fix it," he sighed. "Cam's gone... and that's that."

"But Gia's still out there," Harper insisted, as if helping her parents recall who, in fact, was responsible for their current situation.

"So what?" he cried. "Won't bring my son back."

"You can't tell me you don't want her to pay for what she's done, Dad."

"Of course I do, for Christ's sake. I'd kill her myself if I had half a—"

Bronwyn shot up off the bed as if she had been electrocuted by what her daughter, her husband might be plotting. "Don't you dare!"

Harper shook her head, stunned. "What?"

Bronwyn pointed her finger like it was a sharp knife. "Harper Merritt Langley, do not harm a hair on that witch's head until I have my grandchild in my arms. I mean it! I will never forgive you, and I will never speak to you ever again. I want my grandchild. That baby is all I have left of my son. Do you hear me? After the baby's born I don't give a damn about what happens to that sea demon."

Harper covered her face with her hands.

A sea demon? Harper thought. *How the fuck did we end up here?*

23

December 27th

Gia arrived at the base of the Eiffel Tower in disguise. An auburn wig, a pair of large sunglasses, and a wooly cap hid her identity. She approached the brown awning of the Jules Verne restaurant with supreme caution, hyper vigilant of her surroundings and potential threats. It was then that she was met at the front door by two of Q's men.

"Are you here for *Signor* Mosca?" one asked.

"Unfortunately," Gia chirped, sarcasm thick in her voice.

"This way."

As they entered the restaurant, Gia discovered that Q had paid enough money to clear the place out completely.

How much had that set him back?

People waited months for a reservation—it couldn't have been easy to compensate all those angry patrons overnight. The men escorted Gia into the glass elevator. As it rose, they passed through level after level of the brown iron that Mr. Eiffel had twisted himself.

The men took Gia all the way to a table that was situated in front of the floor-to-ceiling windows.

"Thank you gentlemen," Q said, patting them on the back. "I have asked the chef to set up a table for the two of you in the kitchen. Please enjoy your meal. We will come to you when we are ready to go."

He shuffled toward Gia and took her hand in his. Gia resisted the urge to pull away, her stomach lurched in revulsion to his touch.

"*Signorina* Acquaviva, I have been looking forward to spending time with you since we met in Athens. Feel free to remove your disguise. No one will bother you here."

"I prefer to leave it on," Gia rebuked.

"As you wish. Shall we sit?" Q pulled out Gia's chair for her and settled her in before sitting himself. "I am aware that you do not eat seafood, so I have asked the chef to prepare a meal consisting of your favorite foods."

"How do you know what I like to eat?"

His eyes sparkled as he poured champagne into two square flutes. "Cameron told me." He smiled at the revelation, baring his teeth like a wolf.

Gia leaned forward in her seat and placed her hands on the table, as if getting ready to lunge.

"Cameron? Do you have Cameron?! Where is he right now? Is he in Sicily with Vittore?"

"Do you not watch the news?" Q asked, his eyes narrowing as amusement played at the corners of his mouth.

"What do you mean? What has happened?" Gia demanded.

Q passed her the glass of champagne, but she swatted it away.

"I do not want any goddamn champagne. Tell me what you have done with Cameron."

"Gia, *bella sirena*, this is a 1996 Dom Pérignon Rosé Gold. I will be quite offended if you do not at least have a little toast with me."

"I will toast you after you tell me what I want to know. Now, tell me where Cameron is."

"He took a swim in the Rio di Cannaregio."

"What does that mean?"

"When you did not come to my villa as I requested, I was rather...

displeased. So, he met the same fate that many of your former lovers have. My boys cut his throat and disposed of him in the canal. It is what you would have done, yes?"

Gia covered her mouth to mask her dropped jaw. She was horror-struck and unable to speak. Instinctively, she grabbed her belly, holding onto the last little bit of Cameron that she had left.

Q raised his glass. "To us," he said.

Gia steadied her shaky hand as she tried to process this new reality and touched her glass to his. "*Saluti.*" She took a small sip and was suddenly overwhelmed with nausea. "Excuse me, I am feeling very unwell." She jumped from the table and ran to the ladies room where she proceeded to empty her stomach, which was now filling with grief.

24

December 28th

"Four days ago," Harper spoke to the camera, "my brother's body was found here in a canal in Venice." Her vocal chords grated against each other, and she found it hard to speak with so much tension in her chest. "While you celebrated with your families and held your loved ones close, I visited the local morgue. This is not breaking news. In fact, my brother Cameron's death has already been widely reported. But I have kept my silence over the last few days, trying to process my family's loss."

The camera drew closer to her face, as it appeared that Harper was choking back tears. "What I can promise LION viewers is the truth. I intend to prove that the person who murdered my brother was the same person who murdered Nicolás Ángel Fernández last September. That person is Gia Acquaviva."

The producers cut to the security footage captured from inside Gia's home. On the video, viewers saw Cameron running away from Gia, and then they were sent back to Harper.

"Today, I am bringing you an exclusive sit-down with Paula

Fernández, Nico's sister. We'll be back with Paula right after the break."

The camera light went off, and the station cut to a commercial break.

Harper crossed the studio to an area where the stage had been set with two chairs. Paula was already there—her hands gripped the arms of the seat as she kept her face turned down.

"I do not know if I can do this, Harper," she said, through short, strained breaths.

Harper flagged a production assistant to fetch her handbag and get a glass of water for Paula.

"Give me your hand," Harper commanded gently, placing a pill in Paula's palm. "It's for anxiety. I've been gobbling them up for the last few weeks."

Paula took the water and tossed back the benzo.

"This interview is really going to help me," Harper explained, reassuring Paula. "I do think this will root Gia out, and I want to get my hands on that bitch."

Harper glanced over at the production team and then she squeezed Paula's hand. "Time to get in place. The producer's giving me the signal."

In a moment, the theme music was playing, and the bright light was on Harper once again. She had the producer roll a package about Nico's disappearance, the vigil that had taken place in his honor, and then the discovery of his body.

The interview opened with a close shot on Harper. "Welcome back to Primetime on LION. I'm here with Paula Fernández, Nico's sister." The camera flipped to a wide shot. "Paula, it turns out we have quite a bit in common."

Paula nodded.

"Can you tell me," Harper continued, "what your experience has been with the police here in Venice?"

"It has been shit." Paula threw her hand over her mouth as if surprised by the words she had just blurted out.

"Don't worry, Paula," Harper winked, "there's a little man in an office with his hand on a buzzer ready to bleep out every dirty word. Back to the question. Could you explain why it has been so difficult dealing with the authorities here in Italy?"

"Why? For one thing, the police are corrupt. They protect the criminals. They will not tell you a thing. Harper, I am so thankful to you for your coverage of my brother's case, because if it had not been for you, I would not have known so many of the things you reported."

The camera flashed over to Harper, who had a stern, yet somehow mournful, look on her face. Then back to Paula.

"I miss my brother, desperately. And like you... my mother and I spent Christmas alone for the first time."

Harper reached out and grabbed Paula's hand and held it, as a show of solidarity.

"Should we tell them?" Harper asked Paula.

"Yes."

The camera cut to Harper again. "Paula and I have pooled our resources, and we have put together a fifty thousand dollar reward for any LION viewer who can give us verifiable information about the whereabouts of Gia Acquaviva... but that's not all. We have another twenty five thousand dollars for anyone who can prove corruption within the Venetian police force."

The jib camera swung around and landed close to Harper's face, creating a super dramatic impact. "LION viewers, we're counting on you."

25

December 28th

Her eyes were swollen and red. It took every bit of internal strength Gia had not to fall apart during the flight to Sicily, so the very second she got to her room the prior evening, she lost control of herself. She had cried all night long. Indeed, intense emotion was unfamiliar to her, so she was not entirely sure how to cope with her grief. Her bleary eyes watched the sun stretch awake and rise over Q's lemon grove.

A woman knocked at her door to alert her that breakfast was ready on the terrace. The same two men who had met her at the Eiffel Tower were now stationed outside her door, armed.

"Are you my bodyguards now? Or my jailers?" she barked.

They shrugged.

"What are your names?"

One of the men had a mole on his chin, and the other was bald. The bald one answered first, "Angelo."

"I'm Lorenzo," the other guy said, with a Brooklyn accent.

"You are American?" she asked him.

"Yes, from New York. *Signor* Mosca is my uncle."

"How *lucky* you are," she said, lips tight.

"I think so, ma'am," he replied. "You ready to go up?"

"I can find my own way."

"No, ma'am. I'm sorry, we have instructions to stay with you wherever you go."

"Fine, then first take me to *Signor* Cantalupi's room."

"Who?"

"The old man."

"Oh, he's in the basement. We're not allowed in there."

Angelo elbowed Lorenzo to stop him talking.

"What is in the basement? And why is he there?" Gia's heart raced as her imagination went wild. She would rather die than have something horrible happen to Vittore.

"We better get you up to breakfast," Lorenzo said, staring straight ahead.

They walked together through the vaulted hallways. The smooth stucco walls were covered with large-scale Slim Aarons photos. Q's taste was chic but also cheeky, as evidenced by several off-color Guy Bourdain prints.

Outside, placed on an orange and white striped tablecloth, a breakfast of breads and fruits greeted Gia.

"Good morning!" Q grinned at her and pulled out her chair, as he had done the day before. He acted as if they were on holiday and the oldest of friends.

But she did not sit.

"Where is Vittore?" she demanded.

"Safe and sound. Worry not."

"I want to see him. Bring him up here for breakfast."

"*Signor* Cantalupi takes all of his meals in his room."

"Not anymore," she insisted. "Not while I am in this house."

He exhaled and shook his head, "If it will make you feel more comfortable, fine."

After several minutes that felt like an eternity to Gia, old Vittore was there in front of her. She threw her arms around him.

"Are you all right, *Methusalamme*? I have been very worried about you."

"*Tesoro mio*, I am feeling just fine. Although, I wish you had listened to me and not come."

"How could I leave you here alone? Be serious."

Q interrupted the happy reunion. "Shall we have some breakfast?"

They sat around the table together, and Vittore reached for a few orange slices.

"The one thing I will say about this man," Vittore began, "is that he makes very good lemonade."

Q laughed and Gia let out a smile, in spite of how angry she felt. She squeezed Vittore's frail hand and spoke softly to him. "I cannot tell you how happy I am to see you."

Q ran his fingers through his grey hair and winked at Gia. "I like seeing you happy, *bella sirena*. In fact, I have something special to show you. Something I designed just for you."

He handed her a pair of binoculars.

"Look across the property." He pointed to the other hillside. "Over there."

She lifted the binoculars to see a team of construction workers busy inside a glass box. From her vantage point, it appeared as if they were building a very large sandcastle.

"What am I looking at?" she asked, flatly.

"Your new home. I am aware that you are having a bit of an over-exposure problem at the moment. Killing your high-profile boyfriend does tend to bring unwanted exposure. I thought you might be happy to have a comfortable place to escape."

"Fuck you." The mere allusion to Cameron cut her to the core.

What I would not give to cut his throat right now and end this whole disgusting business.

"Gia," Q's voice was still his signature silky smooth, "Play nice with me. I have gone through the trouble of building the largest aquarium in Europe, just for you."

"An aquarium? That box over there? You expect me to *live there*?

You cannot be serious." Gia's mind raced. *Does he plan to make me a captive in his own private zoo?*

Q blabbered on, as if he wasn't hearing her or didn't care. "You can have the crew make absolutely anything you like... furniture, a ship. They can source aquatic plants—anything you wish. Perhaps we can decide on some of the fish and creatures together?"

This man is absolutely insane. Who could imagine such a thing?

Gia darted her eyes to Vittore, whose face was fixed in disgust, outrage. She patted and stroked Vittore's hand to calm him.

She turned her attention back to Q. "While this is quite an intriguing offer, I must decline. I am not interested in being your spectacle and living in some kind of underwater cage. Frankly, this is bizarre."

Q clucked his tongue in anger and turned to his guard, "I think it might be time to take the old man to meet our doctor downstairs." The guard approached Vittore and pulled his chair out from the table.

"Now, now..." Gia replied, voice unsteady. "We should speak calmly about this. Surely we can reach some kind of arrangement."

"If you value this man's life," Q hissed, "then the decision should be simple."

"Gia," Vittore growled under his breath, "let me go."

She ignored him and instead leveled her eyes at Q. "You are asking a lot, *Signor* Mosca."

Gia bit her lip and tried to stall for time, hoping that inspiration would strike... some genius plan to get them the fuck out of this looney bin. Perhaps the best strategy was to lean into her many charms. After all, she had caught more than her fair share of flies with her signature blend of honey. Maybe if she was pliant enough she could even manage to get him alone.

Gia sighed and then said, "I have not even seen the accommodations up close. Might we have Lorenzo and Angelo take Vittore and myself over there for a short walk?"

Q frowned. "I would rather take you on my own... at least the first time. I would like to introduce you to the architect and the engineer."

"I have been very inconsiderate," Gia noted, lowering her gaze. She could play subservient if that is what tickled this sick man's fancy.

I will have him wrapped around my finger in three days. This is simply a challenge I must meet. I can take control of this situation. And I will.

She raised her eyes to Q and went just shy of fluttering her lashes, "Please, give me the full tour... just the two of us."

26

December 29th

The coroner called Harper sometime after eight o'clock in the evening. Miraculously, the technicians in the lab had returned to the office specifically to process Cameron's test results. There was no telling how much that cost her mother and father. Harper knew they didn't do it out of the goodness of their hearts—Italians did not like being called away from their families to work during the holidays.

Harper rushed over to the coroner's office on a speedboat. Once she got her hands on the report she flipped through it and scoffed, "This is all in Italian!"

"*Signorina* Langley," the coroner replied, "with all due respect, we are in Italy. My sincere apologies. There was no time to have it translated."

"But this is everything?"

"*Sì, sì.*"

"Toxicology, too?

He nodded.

"Explain to me what it all says. I'll take notes."

"The body—"

Harper cut him off. "That body was a person and has a name. Call him *Cameron*, please."

The coroner swallowed unevenly and then began again, "Cameron... ah... as I told you before... he had been transported to the canals after expiring. This is clear because he suffered a significant loss of blood prior to being placed in the water. In addition, the condition of his lungs and the absence of aspiration pneumonia supports that theory. Also... his blood tests revealed a high level of Propofol."

"Is that the drug that they said Michael Jackson used?" Harper tapped away on her Notes app.

"I am not sure what you mean."

"Never mind... go on. What is Propofol?"

"A general anesthetic... normally it is used by doctors during a surgery."

Harper's heart raced.

Why had Gia knocked him out? Harper wondered. *Did she do the same to Nico?*

"Shall I continue?" the coroner asked, hoping so much that the answer would be no.

Harper rolled her hand, indicating that she wanted him to get on with it.

"The wound at his neck was inflicted using a straight blade, likely a razor... possibly a very sharp box cutter."

Harper clenched her jaw and closed her eyes. She wanted to cry, but she kept the feelings locked in her chest. "Continue."

"There are two more very strange things... we found a high concentration of lemon pulp in his stomach."

"Lemons? Cam doesn't even really like lemons."

"The other piece of evidence I cannot yet make sense of... under his toenails we found dirt... and the sample contained volcanic ash. Had he recently been near a volcano?"

"What? A volcano? I have no idea. I hadn't seen him for several weeks. God knows where that woman dragged him. Where did the volcanic ash come from—can you tell?"

"Unfortunately, I cannot," the coroner replied.

* * *

ONCE HARPER GOT SETTLED back into her suite at the Bauman, she rang Paula to come over.

"Paula," she moaned into the phone. "Come get wasted with me. I just got the autopsy report back. Misery needs some company."

Paula showed up half an hour later, carrying a bottle of vodka. After a room-temperature shot, Harper called down to the kitchen for some ice and mixers. After everything was delivered, she made herself a vodka soda. Her hand levitated momentarily over a plate full of lemon slices. She grabbed one and squeezed the life out of it, tossing its crescent-shaped carcass into a nearby wastebasket.

Harper's eyes zoned out as she took a big gulp of her cocktail. Then her mouth ran, practically on its own, "She cut him open with a razor blade. *Slipppf.* Dead... oh, but before that... mmm... she put him to sleep. I hope he didn't feel anything."

"What do you *mean* she put him to sleep?" Paula inquired. "I do not understand this phrase."

"Shot him up with heavy-duty doctor drugs, hospital-grade apparently."

"She used a sedative on your brother?" Paula asked, and then shook her head. "That was not what happened with Nico."

"I never got to see the autopsy, so I wouldn't know. Tried to pay for it... guess I didn't know the *right* person to pay. Of course, good ol' Daddy dear could have helped me... but he left me on my own." She shrugged as she finished her drink and prepped another.

"You mentioned a razor blade. That is different also. My brother's cut was strange... serrated. They were not able to determine what kind of blade was used. They said there was a very unusual pattern to the cut... a scallop shape."

"Mmm... maybe Gia got bored and switched things up." Harper

saw that Paula had finished her drink. "Let me top you off. But first... I think I'll take a little pill, one... maybe two *little*, tiny orange pills. Do you want one?"

"You may find me on the floor after that," Paula admitted.

"That's fine," Harper titled the bottle of vodka into Paula's tumbler, "sleep over."

27

December 28th

The view from inside Gia's soon-to-be prison cell was breathtaking. One-hundred-and-eighty degrees of Sicilian countryside. To the right, the lemon grove and the hillside. To the left, the Mediterranean sea, unusually still today. The sunshine warmed the air, masking a slight chill. The aquarium was four stories high and built into the side of a mountain.

If Q hadn't intended to trap her in it, Gia could have imagined herself admiring the construction. She touched the thick plexiglass with both hands and tried to envision what it would be like once the box was filled with saltwater and locked at the top. She thought of trapped dolphins and sharks in aquariums and how absolutely tragic it was to pull them from their vast network of oceans and confine them to small structures, cutting them off from their world, just for the sake of human amusement.

Gia not only swam in the sea but also roamed the land and explored the skies, so in a way Q's plans to imprison her were even more cruel.

And what will he do to me later? Gia's disquieted mind could not calm itself, and her sense of dread was turning into horror. *Sell tickets for people to come and watch me? Am I supposed to raise my little baby in captivity?*

"What do you think?" Q asked, walking up behind Gia, interrupting her anxious thoughts. She tried to arrange her face into serene lines.

"The view is incredible, truly. Tell me everything you have in mind. I am very interested in all your plans." Her voice sounded calm, but her heart raced.

"What a change in attitude I am observing!" Q obviously wasn't buying what she was selling. She made a mental note to tamp down her false enthusiasm.

"You are a businessman, are you not? If I am to accept your offer, then I must do my due diligence."

"Indeed you must. Now, let me introduce you to the maestros!" He directed her over to two nervous-looking gentlemen. On a folding table sat several sets of blueprints.

She bent over them as the men explained the water filtration system. She eyed the plans for escape routes but found none.

"Eventually," Q told her, "I will build a tunnel out to the sea for a constant flow of fresh saltwater, but to start, I have water trucks coming to fill it, starting in just a few days."

"Water trucks?" Gia repeated. "Where is the water coming from?"

"Believe it or not, the saltwater will come from seas all over Europe. Wherever the trucks are, they will fill up and come here. It is a very complicated operation. Hopefully it will all be ready in three weeks or so." He turned to the engineer. "My friend here is working diligently to complete the project in record time. And we do not foresee any problems, do we?"

"None at all, sir," the man replied.

Gia noticed a pen near the edge of the table and while the men were looking in another direction, she swiped it and slipped it into her bra. She desperately needed to get word to Stavros about where exactly she and Vittore were and what Q was plotting.

She followed the men inside the sandcastle and tapped Q on the shoulder. "Have you shown the aquarium to *La Nonna* yet?"

"All will be revealed on New Year's Eve. She is coming for dinner."

"How lovely," Gia deadpanned.

"I imagine you are very angry with her for bringing Vittore here and luring you in?"

Gia tossed her head to one side. "I am not happy with her, I cannot lie. But she is loyal to you and that counts for something, I suppose. I do have one small request, if I might?"

"Ask it."

"Could we please bring Vittore upstairs? I hate that he is all alone in the basement."

"I think that could be arranged." He looked into her eyes and the corner of his mouth turned up.

"Thank you." She leaned in toward him, but Lorenzo moved closer to them, his hand gripping a holstered gun. "Relax, Lorenzo," Gia purred. "I will not bite him."

Q wagged his finger at her. "They only want to make sure you do not cut me."

"That is fair," she said, with an exaggerated exhale. "But you cannot keep me away from you forever, now can you?"

He lifted her chin with his thumb, "We shall see, *bella sirena*."

28

November 1994

T hree weeks! Starting tomorrow, Pierre would have Gia all to himself for three full weeks. As they ended their call and he hung up, he floated through his 8th Arrondissement apartment and popped a CD into his big stereo system.

Lately he'd become rather obsessed with a neo-Motown group that had topped the charts in the States. They were called Boyz II Men. The jazzy melody of "I'll Make Love to You" filled the living room and pumped into the surround sound speakers on the terrace. He shimmied around the living room and onto the patio, performing all the parts of the four-man harmony. Every time the song ended, he rushed back to replay it.

Everything was coming together for him.

The acquisition of Thumb Generation, his SMS tech company, was the buzz of Euro Telecom. His closing was set for the end of December. Even though he would be paid out in installments—like the good faith deposit he'd used to buy this apartment—the deal would set him up for life. He would never have to work again, unless he wanted to.

And more and more lately, he envisioned himself investing in Gia's companies and traveling the world with her. If she was the brains of her operation, perhaps she would let him be the wallet? There was plenty of time to work out all the details. He knew she was skittish.

That is fine, he thought. *I can bide my time. Gia is worth it.*

In truth, his mind was already scheming. He could use her long work trip to Paris as a sort of induction to their life together as a real couple. Moreover, it was time to introduce Gia to his son, but he wasn't sure she would love that prospect.

Never mind, he spoke to the growing anxiety knocking its way around his head. *This is a detail to be worked out later.*

First things first, if he was going to be hosting Gia for weeks, it was time to fill this fancy crashpad with some furniture. He threw on some pants and jetted over to Roche Bobois for a sofa.

* * *

PIERRE DESCENDED the spiral staircase into La Perle Noire in the mid-afternoon. Gia had asked the driver to drop her at the club instead of going first to Pierre's apartment, which rather annoyed him. However, he'd come to expect that with Gia, work was always her priority.

The house lights shone at mid-level. Being at her club during this time of day really ruined the magic for him. It felt like walking in on your mother wrapping your Christmas presents.

On the stage, Dimitri paraded dancer after dancer in front of Gia. The women all wore corsets and thongs, paired with impossibly high heels. What the club needed, Dimitri had explained to Gia, were women with exactly the same body type, down to breast size and butt shape. Different colored Barbies modeled on a factory line.

Gia followed his guidance, because, after all, this was her first foray into cabaret, whereas Dimitri had traveled the world performing in burlesque troupes. He understood very well what would sell tickets when it came to nude revues.

Pierre cleared his throat to announce his presence. Gia hadn't noticed him standing directly beside her table.

"*Amore*," she said, waving him into the chair beside her, "give me a kiss."

He instantly felt more at ease as he sidled up to her. "How long until you finish with the auditions?" he asked.

Gia glanced down at her antique Rolex. "It is hard to say."

"Shall I take your bags to the apartment?"

"*Amore*, that would be so lovely. Thank you."

"Will you be home in time for dinner?"

"That depends. What are you suggesting we eat?"

"I could boil some lobsters."

"Absolutely not! How disgusting!" she exclaimed, anger clear on her face.

"Oh... I can whip up something else," offered Pierre lamely, feeling confused by her outburst.

"Pasta?"

"Perhaps a risotto?"

"*Delizioso*." She put both hands on his cheeks, placated, and pulled him in for a juicy kiss, her easy demeanor returned.

"Wonderful, my beautiful girlfriend, I shall see you at seven."

"How about nine?"

"I would settle for eight thirty."

She nodded in agreement, and he left.

* * *

THE RISOTTO SAT cold and lonely on the brand new dining table. Pierre had already finished three-quarters of a bottle of white wine all on his own, and, at this late hour, he felt increasingly sour about the whole situation. What he really wanted to do was walk back over to the club and drag Gia home with him, but he knew that would only send her packing.

He frowned at the table, grabbed what remained of the wine, and headed to the upper terrace. Once there, he wrapped his big sweater around his chest and dangled his feet into the hot tub.

Finally, after another twenty minutes or so, he heard footsteps downstairs and several sets of laughter. He felt anger bubble inside of him.

Gia bringing company with her further annoyed him, so rather than heading down to meet her, he stayed up top and sulked. After a few minutes the party found its way to him.

"Here he is!" Gia shouted over her shoulder. She sauntered to the edge of the hot tub and ran her hands through Pierre's hair. "I have been searching for you, *amore*."

"I was here the whole time."

She pouted. "Are you very angry with me?"

Pierre didn't reply.

Dimitri clattered his way up the stairs and onto the terrace. He held the pot of risotto and a bottle of champagne. Behind him strode Marion, one of the dancers from the audition. She carried four glasses.

"Dimitri," Gia said, "Pierre is quite upset. I left him alone all night, *poverino*."

"There is only one solution for this very serious problem," Dimitri replied. "We will have to get him good and drunk." He sat the food and alcohol down and began unbuttoning his pants.

"You are too late." Pierre waved his hand at an empty wine bottle. "Already drunk."

Dimitri filled the four champagne flutes. "Then we must all do our best to catch up." He offered Pierre a sly smile, full of promise. Promise of what, Pierre did not know.

Gia dipped a spoon into Pierre's risotto and took a big bite. "*Delizioso!*"

"It was much better when it was hot," Pierre muttered.

"To Pierre," Dimitri said, raising his glass, "thank you for allowing us to crash your romantic evening. Now, everyone, please lose the clothes and get into this jacuzzi to cheer up our host."

Pierre watched his guests fully disrobe. Once they were all naked, he shyly slipped off his own clothes and hopped under the bubbles. Gia climbed in beside him, sat down on Pierre's lap, and kissed him softly. She whispered, "I am sorry, *amore*," before turning her attention to Marion, beckoning her over. "Pierre, please let our new friend try some of your risotto." Gia filled the spoon and gave it to Pierre. "Open up," she directed Marion.

Pierre squinted his eyes in Gia's direction, but Gia had her gaze trained on Marion's naked body.

"Me first!" Dimitri splashed in front of Marion and curled his lips around Pierre's spoon. "Mmmm," he said as he chewed. "Pierre, give me one more bite, please."

Pierre obliged. As he brought the spoon to Dimitri's mouth, Dimitri wrapped a hand around Pierre's wrist and guided the spoon deep inside. Pierre's thumb grazed Dimitri's lips on the way in. Dimitri sucked the spoon dry and swallowed.

Gia reached into Pierre's lap and stroked him. "Come here, Dimitri," Gia commanded. She gently encouraged Pierre to sit on the side of the hot tub and pushed Dimitri's head into Pierre's lap.

"Ahh, umm, I don't know about this..." Pierre shifted uncomfortably in his seat.

Gia called the woman over with the wag of one finger. "Would you rather have her mouth on your cock?"

Dimitri had already wrapped both hands and his tongue around Pierre. To Pierre's surprise, he found himself very hard, and he decided to go with it. After all, this was what Gia wanted him to do, so why not? It was exciting.

He relaxed and let his head fall back. Gia kissed his neck. Marion paddled over to Pierre's right side and bit his earlobe. Thank God Pierre was distracted by the overstimulation, because otherwise he would have come—and come hard.

29

New Year's Eve

A waxing crescent moon dangled in the cloudless sky. Gia tried opening the window in her room at Q's villa, but it was locked. Breaking the window was out of the question, as armed guards stood in the courtyard. In the room next to hers, she heard a different set of guards shuttle Vittore into his new lodging.

At least she was able to bring him a little comfort, regardless of whatever might happen later.

When the door closed in Vittore's room, he began calling for Gia. She rushed to a grate in the wall where she could whisper to him.

"Come here, *Methusalamme*," she ordered, "they are probably listening to us, possibly watching us. So keep quiet."

"But *tesoro mio*, what can we do… you cannot stay here. Especially not in your condition."

"Hush up, old man. Trust me. I have a plan."

"I was a fool to leave Stavros. I should not have trusted *La Nonna*."

Silently, she agreed with him. But it would not do any good to reprimand him for his error.

Gently, she replied, "You will see him soon enough. I do not want another word about it. Now, get some sleep."

"I love you, Gia."

"I love you, too, *Methusalamme*."

Gia sashayed over to the closet and slid through every hanger, eyeing the clothes Q had bought for her and placed there. A paper tag hung off a white silk dress. It read: *"per la Cenone di Capodanno"*—for New Year's Eve dinner.

She pulled it off the rack.

It was a mermaid-cut gown, nipped at the waist and tight until just above the knee. Scalloped neckline.

Mermaid dress for the mermaid... at least the man has a sense of humor, Gia thought.

She needed to summon as much sex appeal as possible and try to win him over. Gia ripped off the tag and laid it on the bedside table. She stepped into the dress and lifted it over her hips. Once it was over her cleavage, she began to close the hidden zipper on the side hem, but it got caught at her belly.

"Merda," she cursed to herself. She lowered the dress and saw that she could cut the fabric of the lining to allow herself just enough room to zip the dress closed. She winced as her gills lifted from beneath her muscles and emerged from her right forearm. She used the serrated edges to make little rips in the fabric and finished tearing it by hand, sighing with relief once the zipper was firmly closed under her arm.

Now, the tag. Gia smiled to herself. *How useful.*

She jotted a few sentences on it and rolled it up into a neat, tiny cylinder and hid it under her dress.

* * *

"AH, AND HERE SHE IS," Q looked ever so much like a Bond villain in his white tuxedo jacket. "Donatella," he turned his attention to *La Nonna*, "you will be glad to know that Gia has confessed to me that she is not angry with you."

"What a relief," she said, with a hefty helping of sarcasm. "Truly, I was holding my breath."

"Good evening," Gia said approaching *La Nonna*. "Why not shake hands and be friends again?"

La Nonna pursed her lips in puzzlement and extended her hand. Gia clasped the outstretched hand with both of hers and pressed the note into *La Nonna*'s palm. The old woman took it without missing a beat and stashed it in her pocket.

"*Madonna!*" *La Nonna* laughed. "Perhaps you have met your match in *Signor* Mosca. You are quite changed, *angioletta*." She leaned in closer and lowered her voice a bit, "I am sorry about Cameron."

Gia winked. "All is fair in love and war, no? Q simply saved me having to do it myself. What *is* unfortunate is that he robbed me of the pleasure of it." Gia cast her gaze to Q and found him to be utterly transfixed by her.

A few members of staff came to seat the ladies and shake martinis for the table.

The waiter passed a stemmed glass to Gia, but she turned him down. Looking directly at *La Nonna*, Gia said, "I am not drinking for the next few months."

"Why is that?" Q inquired.

Gia shrugged. "Watching my figure," she said, offering an explanation for abstaining.

The staff served the entrées, and after some idle chit-chat, Gia took a deep breath and began the evening's real conversation. "I have been giving this some thought, Q, and I would like to accept your offer to live here, on one condition."

La Nonna perked up. "*Signor* Mosca has invited you to *live* here?"

"Oh yes," she flashed a smile that she knew *La Nonna* would read as fake. "Did he not tell you? He has built Europe's largest aquarium *just* for me."

La Nonna burst into laughter, but quickly stopped when she realized that neither Q nor Gia were laughing. "Ah," she said, "that sounds like quite an undertaking." She demurely chugged her martini and signaled for another.

"What is your one condition before you accept my generous offer?" Q asked, spreading caviar on a fresh blini.

Gia eyed the fish eggs and tried not to frown. She lifted her eyes and squared them with Q's. "I will stay here if you let Vittore return to Venice."

"Hmm," he said, swallowing. "What do you think of this offer, Donatella?"

She took a long time to answer. Too long.

Q swizzled the olives in his martini. "Please share your thoughts, Donatella. We are both anxious to hear what Italy's best deal-maker has to say."

La Nonna glanced at Gia and tried not to wince. "I think, *Signor* Mosca, that you know very well what I have to say about it. One never accepts the first offer."

Under the table Gia dug her nails into the chair, she should have known this would not be as easy as she had hoped.

"Sweeten the deal for me, then, Gia," Q smirked.

"Amalfi," Gia answered instantly. "When we met, you mentioned that you liked my Amalfi club the most. It can be yours."

Q arched back into his chair. "Now things are becoming more interesting."

The staff removed the first-course plates and served a palate cleanser, a small ball of sorbet, made with lemons from the grove.

"Tell me," *La Nonna* began, "will Gia live in the tank full time or will she travel for work?"

"What a strange question," Q replied evenly. "Why would she ever want to leave? And anyway... is she not wanted for *murder*? How many murders are the police trying to pin on you, Gia? If I were her... ha! I would take the opportunity to hide forever."

"However, Donatella makes an excellent point, Q," Gia countered. "I cannot possibly run the whole business remotely."

"Of course not," he said, licking the last bit of sorbet from the tiny spoon. "Which is why you will sign everything over to me."

La Nonna felt a hot surge of regret bounce through her chest and land in her gut. She had seen women come into Q's life and disappear, but locking Gia in a fishbowl? It was cruel and absurd. Cumulatively, it was becoming clear to her that there were no lines he would not cross, no act too depraved. After all, he was ready to kill her simply for failing to deliver Gia in a timely fashion.

The thought of usurping his power or somehow diminishing his influence had continued to grow in her mind like a noxious weed.

But how could I remove him from his throne? That question had been echoing in *La Nonna's* head rather constantly lately.

It would not be a simple task—of that she was sure.

Gia balked at Q's brazen greed, "You expect me to give you everything?"

"Unless you prefer a painful death for your old friend," Q quipped.

Vittore was more important to Gia than anything. What choice did she have? He was her only connection to the past, to a happy adolescence. He was her only source of comfort and care for thirty years—a father, really. She could never allow him to suffer, no matter the cost to her.

"How can I guarantee that you will not kill him anyway?"

"*Bella sirena*, if you agree to this deal, I will let him leave tonight with Donatella."

She didn't give it a moment's thought. "Then I agree. Yes."

Q clapped his hands together. "Wonderful! I love it when everything works out as planned."

30

New Year's Day

"Wishing you a very Happy New Year..." drolled a woman with a Kentucky accent, "from all of us at OTN. This is Ashley Mason, and I am coming to you live from New York with an exclusive on the Mermaid case that's been a global sensation since before Christmas... and yes... at OTN we say *Christmas*! What you're gonna find here at OTN is the simple truth, and not all that P.C. bullcrap. To that I say... thank God for OTN!"

Royce and Bronwyn stood behind the lead camera, observing Ashley. When Harper left them for LION, they quickly pulled the bleach blonde off the flagging morning show and placed her in the prime time slot. So far, the audience was responding well. According to the ratings, it appeared that they liked her ultra-conservative, liberal-hating approach to the news.

"Last week, our competitor put up a reward for Gia Acquaviva. Folks, I can now tell you that OTN is upping that offer, and we will give two hundred and fifty thousand dollars for information that leads to the *safe* return of Gia Acquaviva."

Ashley shuffled notecards at the anchor desk, pulling out one specific card. "You all know that this case is close to the heart of our incredible leader here at OTN... Cameron Langley was Royce Langley's son. The next piece of information has not yet been shared *anywhere*. Royce Langley wants Gia returned unharmed! Gia is pregnant with his son's child. Yes, you heard that right. *She is pregnant.* Royce wants to make sure Gia is safe and that his first little grand-baby is safe, too. So whatever you do, be careful. This quarter-of-a-million dollar reward goes away... *poof*... if any harm comes to Gia Acquaviva. Happy hunting, folks! But be delicate! A precious child's life is at stake here!"

31

January 2nd

Stavros threw his arms around Vittore and squeezed him tightly. "I took the first flight I could book to Venice," Stavros cried. "That damned ferry from the airport was late. Oh, my lover... I have nearly lost my mind worrying about you. Are you all right? Did they hurt you in any way?"

"Bah!" Vittore sputtered. "Only a bit of acid on the stomach from all the lemonade. I am well. But what is making me feel sick is that Gia is still there with that monster. He wants to lock her into an aquarium. An aquarium! Can you imagine?"

"An aquarium? Where?!" Stavros replied, trying to make sense of this new information.

"He built an enormous tank at his villa! He is a sick individual. We cannot leave Gia there. We must think of a way to get her out. How can we do it? Will her family in Greece help us?"

Stavros tried to imagine the prison that Gia was facing and inhaled sharply, "That I cannot say. The excommunication order has been signed." He shook his head, as if making a decision. "Here is the truth... I do not care one clamshell if they want to boot me from their underwater country club! I have always charted my own path, and I will continue to live as I please!"

"Ah! Gia left a note with *La Nonna*. *La Nonna* came to me yesterday and gave me the note. I could not read it, because it is in Greek. She must have meant it for you. We have to do something, because *La Nonna* said our time is running out. That lunatic is filling up his aquarium, and he will put my Gia in it. Let me get the note for you." He hobbled to a cabinet and removed the note from a book where he'd hidden it.

Stavros took it in his hand. "Pass me your glasses, please. These old eyes are good only for seeing your face."

Vittore handed over the reading glasses with a kiss. Stavros looked at the note and then said, "This is Atargatis, not Greek." He read the note aloud, translating as best he could from Atargatis to Italian, "Heed the warning of Laocoon when rolling metal horses are pregnant with water from the sea."

"What does it mean?" Vittore wondered aloud. "Father in the Sky! She needs to be rescued and she sends this riddle instead."

"Yes," Stavros said, pulling on his beard, "it is a riddle... and we must uncover the meaning. Let me think. Laocoon... hmm... he was a soothsayer in ancient times, I believe. Metal horses. *Rolling* metal horses... that is the real mystery."

"I would like to travel to your colony and demand help," Vittore insisted.

"Unfortunately that will not be allowed. We must receive an invitation from Queen Zale. When Gia called me to tell me she was going to Sicily to free you, I sent word to my queen, but so far she has not responded. Gia also told me that the Senegalese Queen would lend her support. Gia had a plan, you see... she was not sure what would happen to her, but she said that I should contact Queen Awa in Senegal for help. I have requested an audience with her immediately after I spoke to Gia, and I received word this morning that she has accepted and is awaiting our arrival in Dakar. I think the best course of action is to start there while we wait for word from Queen Zale in Greece."

"Then shall we fly to Senegal?" Vittore asked, his eyes shining.

"Yes, my young love. But I do fear for your safety. We should not travel alone. Let me call my sons and grandchildren to come. If this *Signor* Mosca is the beast you say he is, then we will need protection."

32

January 7th

Someone lightly rapped at Gia's door. It wasn't mealtime, and anyway, the housekeeper never knocked; Lornezo or Angelo just popped the door open and let her in. Gia figured it was Q, and she was right.

He strode into her room, rolling a suitcase.

"Are you bored?" he asked. "I imagine you must be after five days alone."

She ignored his question. "Did Vittore make it back to Venice? Is he all right?"

"The old man is just fine. Shame you two could not say goodbye before Donatella took him away."

"No. It is better... he would not have agreed to leave had he seen me."

"How sweet," Q replied sarcastically.

"Are you going somewhere?" Gia inquired, pointing at Q's suitcase.

"This is for you."

"Ah, so you are setting me free."

Q chuckled. "You can be funny sometimes... a bleak sense of humor. I like that."

"I am glad I amuse you."

Gia glanced at the door. Lorenzo was keeping watch on them. She considered slicing Q's throat then and there, but, no doubt, she would be shot on the spot. Furthermore, she could not be sure what would happen to Vittore if she were to die, so she decided it was better not to tempt fate.

"Have you been to the Maldives?" Q asked, pushing the suitcase over to the closet.

"No," she lied.

Of course she had been to the Maldives, for God's sake. Who hadn't? She'd taken a former lover there, a singer. After that trip, he never sang again.

"I would like to see that tail of yours in action," Q said, unzipping the bag.

* * *

ON Q's JET, Gia wasn't left alone for a second. It wasn't just Lorenzo and Angelo anymore either. Q had brought a whole crew of men. They filled up half the plane. It practically felt like they were flying commercial... apart from the chic interior and chef-prepared meals. There was a full kitchen on his plane, after all.

Gia strategized how she might get away. She figured she would have to be patient, get Q to trust her and then earn some alone time with him. Then, she'd lunge at him. How long would it take to win him over completely? She'd wrapped famous men around her finger before in mere moments.

"Q," she said, nudging his foot with hers. He was sitting across from her, engrossed in a novel. "If we are to spend some time together, then why not get to know each other better? Tell me about yourself."

He laid the book down on his tray table. "What would you like to know about your illustrious host?"

"What were you like as a little boy?" In her experience, men loved to reminisce about their boyhoods.

"I was ambitious."

"Interesting," she replied. "How so?"

"If you are hoping to learn about how I became the man I am today, I hate to disappoint you, Gia. I do not share my secrets."

"A man of mystery, then?"

He nodded and clucked, "Precisely."

"Did you ever consider marriage... a family?"

"I was married... once."

"I see."

"But we share a similar habit, *bella sirena*."

"Meaning?"

"We enjoy killing our lovers."

Somehow, when he declared the obvious, it filled Gia with disgust. She wasn't anything like him. Was she?

"And what about children?"

"I tried that as well," he said, with a faraway look.

"What happened?"

"It is much less satisfying than killing the mother."

* * *

THE JET TOUCHED down at Hanimaadhoo Airport in the late afternoon. Gia and Q's squad boarded a yacht and whirled through the pristine water until they reached a private island. A semi-circle of eco-luxe cabins was wrapped around a turquoise bay.

Gia was assigned the center residence, and beside her teak villa was Q's. The front porch featured an infinity pool that jutted up to the water. The staff at the retreat fetched two hammocks for Lorenzo and Angelo. The boys were stationed to block her only exit.

At sunset, Q retrieved Gia and swept her off to a beachside fire pit to eat dinner. He was always careful to stay out of striking range.

Later, when the sky was lit with a half moon and countless stars, he gave her instructions.

"Undress and swim in the bay for me," Q ordered Gia. "I have waited long enough for this."

She turned away from him and unbuttoned her linen shirt.

"Face me," he commanded.

She did as he asked. Once she took off her shirt, there was no hiding her belly anymore.

"Are you... hmm. Yes, I think you are. You are pregnant."

She squeezed her eyes shut and didn't answer.

"Cameron is the father?"

Gia lowered her head.

"How interesting," Q mused. "He did not mention a baby. He must have loved you."

"And I loved him," she answered, honesty thick in her voice.

Q's eyes flashed with jealousy. "Get in the water."

She trod on the soft sand into the warm water. Diving to the bottom of the shallow bay, she saw that there was a gap between the floating docks housing the villas and the floor of the sea. As her scales pushed through her skin, she was able to swim faster and faster. She dipped under the villas and hit open water at a good clip.

33

November 1994

Pierre waited outside the backdoor at La Perle Noire. Beside him was Marion, wearing a bedazzled beret and smoking a cigarette. Gia, as usual, was late. The door swung open and out popped Dimitri's head.

"Marion," Dimitri fussed, "no smoking until your set is over. You know the rules."

She sighed with frustration at being interrupted and dropped the cigarette, stamping it out with her pink stiletto.

Pierre hadn't seen Dimitri since they got to know one another more intimately in the hot tub. His hands felt clammy and his throat was dry.

"*Bonsoir*," Dimitri said to Pierre, as he stepped into the chilly alleyway. They air-kissed on both cheeks, Dimitri lingering as he planted the second kiss on Pierre's cheek. "How are you?"

"Ah... fine. Y—you?" Nerves and awkwardness were palpable in Pierre's voice.

"For crying out loud," Dimitri scoffed, rolling his eyes, "you are not the first *straight guy* to have his dick sucked by another man. Relax."

The door squeaked open again, and much to Pierre's relief, Gia exited this time.

She smiled at them. "Look at this. My two favorite boys together." She pecked Dimitri on the lips and then wrapped her arms around Pierre and gave him a deep, warm kiss. "*Amore*, shall we go?"

"Where are you headed?" Dimitri asked.

"You, *bello*, are not invited... not tonight. Pierre has a surprise for me."

"And we are very late already," Pierre said, pulling Gia close to him, "so we should leave now."

Dimitri pouted.

"*Tsk, tsk,*" Gia walked over to Dimitri and put her finger on his nose. "Do not worry, *bello*, we are not finished with you."

"Not yet, anyway," Dimitri replied.

Gia kissed him under his ear and whispered, "Dimitri, come to the apartment tomorrow night." Then she turned and took Pierre's hand and they departed, rounding the corner together.

Once they were out of Dimitri's sight, Pierre pushed Gia against the wall and kissed her neck. "I do not enjoy watching you kiss him, Gia."

Gia ran her hand along the front of his wool coat and opened a button, slipping her hand inside to touch his pants. "It seems you do like it... quite a lot, actually."

She was right, and he knew it. His face burned hot. "Stop teasing me."

"Never." Gia bit his lower lip and fumbled with the zipper on his pants.

"We have to go," he groaned.

"Who cares? They will give our table away."

"Everyone is waiting for us."

Gia tensed and pulled back. "Everyone?" she questioned.

Pierre grimaced. "I want you to meet my son. Tonight is his birthday... so, you see, we really must go now, before we ruin the night for him."

"You want me to meet *your son*?" She was taken aback, as she had not expected this, and more than that, the prospect of a night with some kid sounded highly unappealing.

"Is that so bad?"

Gia buttoned the top button on her leather jacket and began walking down the street. "Why did you not mention this before? I was not aware you had a child."

"He is a man now. Today he is eighteen."

"Pierre..." Gia avoided eye contact. "I am not... a family-oriented person."

"Will it hurt you to try? Please? I promised to introduce him to the woman I love."

Gia grabbed him by the lapel and pulled him in to glare at him, her eyes flashing. "I could kill you. I really could."

Pierre offered her a nervous smile, no doubt underestimating the weight of her words. "Would you mind holding off on murdering me until the end of the evening?"

* * *

GIA AND PIERRE stepped into Le Petit Bateau. Over their heads, red lanterns swung in the belly of the boat. Half pirate ship, half tourist trap, the restaurant was incredibly packed with college students. Pierre took Gia by the hand as they ducked into the VIP room, which was situated in the wheelhouse.

"Papa!" Pierre's son waved him over.

"Where is your mother?"

"You missed her," he replied. The young man's eyes landed on Gia, and he mouthed to himself, "*Putain, elle est magnifique.*"

"Gia," Pierre said, "this is my son, Florent."

"*Florent?*" Gia tossed her head to the side, glaring at Pierre. "Florent, really?"

Pierre shrugged, looking sheepish.

"Florent," Gia said to Pierre's son, "when I met your father he told me *his* name was Florent."

"It was the first name that came to my mind! What can I say for myself? You had me tongue-tied," Pierre explained, laughter in his voice.

Florent wrested a bottle of scotch away from his friends and poured a glass for Gia.

"Nothing for your old man?" Pierre teased.

"Old men can fend for themselves!" Florent winked and lifted his glass to touch Gia's.

"*Saluti,*" she said, looking into Florent's shining eyes, "*buon compleanno.*"

Pierre slid his hand onto the small of Gia's back. He felt completely at peace and plum proud. Gia was quite a gleaming gem to show off. He knew Florent was impressed. Too bad his ex-wife had missed the spectacle. "Son, pour me a glass of that liquor that I am paying an arm and a leg for."

Florent looks very much like Pierre, Gia thought, *only less worn.*

It was as if every prominent feature of Pierre's had been slightly tweaked, made a bit more symmetrical, and the overall effect was, well, nothing short of remarkably handsome.

As Pierre leaned in to kiss her, Gia wished, instead, that Florent were in his place.

34

January 8th

Gia swam northwest without stopping. Her mind spin-cycled through plans. *How far is it from the Maldives to Sri Lanka?* She tried to chart a path to freedom in her thoughts. *Six hundred nautical miles? A thousand?*

If she swam for a week straight, maybe she would hit solid ground.

As a mermaid who had spent the vast majority of her life on land, she felt very uncomfortable, very exposed, in the water like this. If she could make it to Sri Lanka, then maybe she could find someone to help her. Maybe she could contact Vittore and get him out of harm's way... have him hide somewhere. Maybe in a colony somewhere with Great Uncle Stavros?

She hoped that Stavros had already gotten hold of Vittore and taken him far away. But no matter what was happening with Vittore, the odds were not in her favor. She had no money, no clothes, and no means of transportation, apart from her legs and tail.

What she didn't know was that Q was catching up to her—and fast. He'd sent boats, divers, and drones to seek her out.

Q shouted instructions to the coast guard captain that he'd bribed, "I want a report every five minutes. Whoever finds her first and brings her back to me gets one hundred thousand euros, cash."

The massive crew searched for almost thirty hours when a two-man team—marines from the Maldives National Defense Force—spotted her. They radioed all nearby boats to form a perimeter and drop scuba troops. Gia had managed to swim more than fifty miles before she got caught in a trawling net.

The marines fished her out of the water and tied her up in their boat. One of them snapped a photo to send to his buddies.

"Can you believe this?" one guy said to the other. "A fucking mermaid. Best mission ever. We might as well retire now... we have hit the peak, my friend."

When the men handed Gia over to Q, he thanked them and had his guard fetch fresh cash from the safe. He promptly paid the bounty he owed. And Gia was right back to where she started: under her captor's unmoving thumb.

Q's face was red, and the veins in his neck bulged. "If you try to escape again," he hissed, "I will cut off your tail. Remember Gia, you are pregnant. I imagine there is a *sirenetta* in your belly... so after the baby is born I will still have the mermaid I need for my aquarium."

Even with all the dough Q had splashed around in the Maldives, he knew his crew couldn't stay there. The media was hunting Gia, and if even one person squeaked, he knew it would be game over. Besides, there was work to do. He needed to recoup some losses, and he knew just the place to do that.

Before they could blink, Gia and the whole team were back up in the sky. Leaving the Maldives behind lifted Q's spirits.

Gia looked out the jet window. She felt very disoriented; maybe it was all that time underwater.

"Are we going back to Sicily?" she whispered to Lorenzo.

Instead, Q answered. "I am feeling quite lucky today. While I am not normally a gambling man, I find myself rather eager to become a casino owner... and since we are already on the right side of the world—"

"Ah, so we are flying to Macau," Gia interrupted.

"And why not?" Q powered his seat back and settled into a lie-flat position for a nap.

* * *

It was late morning when the jet arrived in Macau. A dry day, pleasantly warm in the sunshine, the city was seven times the size of Las Vegas. With its giant hotels and uniquely-shaped skyscrapers, Macau was the playground of Asia's many millionaires and billionaires. Interestingly, Macau drew particular criticism from the Mermaid community, since two-thirds of its urban sprawl was built on land "reclaimed" from the sea. Man was not content to fish in the ocean, and increasing greed meant more and more of the water became home to artificial islands.

Nonetheless, wherever Gia saw money, she carved a seat at the table for herself. If there was cash to be made on stolen land, well, her mantra was hate the game, not the player. It took her years to get permission to lease the land for her casino and then to refurbish the tattered building. Athena, Gia's gambling house, was by no means Macau's biggest casino, but it was sizeable and sexy.

Her establishment had a sensual ambiance and a loyal customer base. Plus, with the private champagne room, it was also a speakeasy for strippers. Only highly vetted, high-net-worth individuals were allowed access to the Cherry Playroom. The exotic dancers who won coveted residencies at Athena could squirrel away a quarter of a million dollars in tips in mere months. Of course, nothing came for free, and it wasn't only lap dances bringing in cash for the biggest hustlers, blow jobs over lines of blow were the real money-maker.

Q's driver pulled up to the front of Athena, and oddly, they discovered there were no reporters outside. The place was empty and chained up, just like all of Gia's bars and clubs the world over. It was depressing for Gia to see the casino this way. When she had ordered Yiannis to temporarily close everything, she hadn't stopped to visualize what her request would actually look like. To see her many years of hard work seemingly die off in so little time felt like an enormous failure.

Q and his team were pleasantly surprised to find the place deserted. They had devised a whole plan to smuggle Gia past the media.

Why are there no reporters here? Gia wondered.

Q pieced it together in his mind. While they were still in the air, he had received an alert that a photo had gone viral: Gia in the Maldives. Camera crews from all over the world had swarmed all fourteen airports in the Maldavian Archipelago when the photo was released. Undoubtedly, Q's team had missed the onslaught by a narrow margin of only a few hours. His keen intuition, as usual, had rewarded him handsomely.

Regardless of the lack of people and press at the doors, the security detail still took precautions entering the building. Once inside, Q leaned against a roulette table and cracked a smile. "*Bella sirena*, would you mind showing me to the safe?"

"Safe?" Gia let out a defiant snicker. "I have vaults... multiple."

"Even better."

They meandered through velvet draped rooms before descending several levels to the vaults. She entered the codes, one by one, from memory, and the pneumatic doors slid open, exposing a significant portion of her fortune to these pirates.

"You are aware," Gia began, "that you will need this cash to run this casino? I can appreciate that the obvious might not be clear to a novice."

"Ah," Q clicked tongue on his teeth, "but you see, I do not plan to operate this business. No, no... Macau is much too far from Italy. Is that not how Rome fell? By extending the empire too far? I intend to sell this place."

Gia leaned against the wall and crossed her arms. "Then you are even more naive than I realized."

"How bold you are," he said. "Watch your disrespectful tone with me. You do not want me getting angry with you, now do you?"

"I only mean to explain that real estate transactions here are extremely complicated. Ever more so, now that China seems intent on exerting increasing control over the autonomous regions. You will need a special grant to transfer the land lease, which may take a long, long time."

"We have Donatella," Q replied. "She is quite capable of retaining local counsel and closing any deal. I am confident."

"I suppose we shall see," Gia replied, looking off into the air. She knew that there was no way he'd be able to land a deal without her personal contacts.

"Hopefully we will not encounter legal problems in Buenos Aires."

"Buenos Aires?"

"Oh, yes, *bella sirena*. I told you already, I have no intention of doing business outside of Europe. I already have a friend interested in taking over all of your businesses in South America."

35

January 9th

"Breaking news," Harper announced as she spoke into the microphone outside Gia's palazzo. "I can confirm that LION has obtained a new photograph of my brother's alleged killer, Mermaid Gia Acquaviva."

The producers cut to the cell phone pic captured by the giddy marine. A friend of a friend of a friend had received the forwarded image and called LION to claim the reward.

In the photo, Gia's hands were bound, and her wet hair was draped over her body. Her white tail stretched out the back of a boat. The poor woman was the picture of despair.

"This photo was taken yesterday in the Maldives... a group of islands in the Indian Ocean. Gia is a long way from home. Unfortunately, shortly after her capture, Gia was released. We don't know why, but we are working around the clock to uncover the full story. What you'll see over the next few days is all the other networks rushing to the Maldives... and listen... I'm all for thorough reporting, so more power to them. We will use all the information they gather... *but* what I know about Gia is that she moves very fast. LION isn't going to be sending our crews to the Maldives on a fishing expedition or some network-sponsored beach vacation. No, we are keeping our eyes on the prize... we have camera crews scattered all over the world, because we know that Gia could resurface *anywhere*."

To the left of Harper's shoulder, a graphic of a stack of money appeared.

"Our fifty thousand dollar reward was awarded to the person who sent this photo to LION. However, the very generous owner of LION... Mr. Goldie Stern... has very kindly offered a new reward. And it far exceeds the current reward by a *competitive* network."

The main camera zoomed in on Harper, capturing a close shot of her face. "Mr. Stern and the network are offering five hundred thousand dollars to any LION viewer who can bring my brother's alleged killer to justice. Unlike our competitors, LION is willing to pay that reward regardless of whether Gia Acquaviva is dead or alive."

36

"What does the real estate agent say?" Pierre asked Gia. On the terrace of his fancy crashpad, they soaked up what little evening sun Paris had to offer huddled under a heat lamp. Pierre sipped red wine.

"She said there is already an all-cash bid for the Amalfi property I want."

"So bid higher," he insisted.

She pushed back from the table and stood, turning her back on Pierre.

"Gia, if you need additional capital, I would love to help you." He rose and hugged her from behind. "Truth be told, I have been hoping for this moment."

"Is that so?" Gia wasn't the least bit surprised. Pierre was suffocating her. Every day the urge to slit his throat and feel him crumble into her arms grew stronger. Sometimes the fantasy of killing him was the only thought that helped her reach climax during solo sex.

He stroked her hair and said, "The next payout for the acquisition will not be made until January, but I already have another solution lined up."

She leaned against his shoulder, feigning interest in him and keeping quiet.

"I will sign this apartment over to you, and you can use it as collateral on a line of credit. I have already spoken to my banker, and he assures me that there will be no issue getting cash for you."

"I have never had an investor," Gia whispered. "I am not sure I want to start now."

"Do not think of me as an investor, *mon amour*. See the additional capital as an expression of my love for you. I have more money coming next year. With my help you can finally achieve one of your biggest dreams. How happy do you think this makes me?"

The doorbell chimed.

"Are we expecting company?" Pierre asked.

"Only Dimitri."

"Oh." Pierre felt disappointed at not having more time alone with Gia. Deeper down, though, the prospect of another night with Dimitri intrigued him. "Then I will open another bottle of red."

As they gathered, Gia chatted away with Dimitri in Greek, sharing this and that about the club—a bit of gossip, a few items of business. Pierre didn't really mind. He had gotten used to their banter and no longer felt left out. On the contrary, his life had never been quite so animated. Lately, he felt as if he was living in a Bertolucci film.

Pierre leaned over Dimitri's shoulder and poured him a glass of wine. Dimitri angled his head up and smirked. "Is it just me, or are you in an excellent mood this evening?"

Pierre laughed.

"He laughs!" Dimitri gulped his wine.

"Perhaps I am happy to see you?"

"Ah, are you?"

"Are *you* happy to see me?" Pierre pulled a stool to the kitchen island next to Dimitri.

"Gia," Dimitri fanned himself with one hand, "am I blushing?"

"Maybe a little," she winked.

"So, Dimitri," Pierre leaned in, "tell me everything scandalous happening in your life right now."

Dimitri lifted an eyebrow. "Have you been body snatched, Pierre?"

"Not remotely. I am settling into bohemia."

His comment made Gia and Dimitri burst into laughter. They tried many times—and failed—to stop their hysterics. What made things worse was that Pierre wasn't laughing, so the whole thing felt even more hilarious to them.

When they finally began to settle down, Pierre interjected, "I am quite serious." This had the opposite effect he desired and spurred them to begin another round of laughter, seemingly at Pierre's expense.

To show he meant business, Pierre took the wine glass out of Dimitri's hand and placed it on the counter. Then, he spun the bar stool around, turning Dimitri toward him. Pierre squared himself between Dimitri's knees and lowered his head, resting his lips inches from Dimitri's. "Now, does it seem like I am joking?"

37

January 9th

Days into their stay at the Coral Tower, Vittore, Stavros, and the family were all anxious for the arrival of Queen Awa. Having failed to secure funding in Hong Kong for her son, Queen Awa was equally anxious to return to Dakar.

The whole business about Gia was extremely messy, and the Queen almost regretted pledging her help after Gia's trial in Santorini. At the same time, there was much to be gained from an alliance with Gia.

Unlike the Greeks, isolated in their underwater maze of caverns, Queen Awa had encouraged her subjects to interface regularly with the humans of Senegal and live double lives.

Did the Queen have concerns about and contempt for Man?

Yes, of course.

But she was of the mind that it was better to live among one's enemy to understand their weaknesses. Queen Awa had learned much in her two-hundred-year reign.

The Queen had protected her subjects during the enslavement of more than ten million people from the African continent. She had observed the rise of the Greek mermaids as their colony became the financial center of the Atargatic world. And more recently, she was witnessing the destruction of the planet by Man, the raping of the oceans. Man spat in the eye of the Gracious Tides—and yet—Man was ignorant that the sea owns the Earth. Those who rise against the sea are drowned.

Queen Awa knew that while Gia was half Man, her soul was entirely Atargatic. With her vast fortune, Gia could prove to be the perfect ally in Man's increasingly hostile and volatile world.

After an evening of rest in her chambers, Queen Awa and her Queen Consort, Ndeye, called a meeting in the Nautilus Dome. Inspired by the architectural sculptures of Richard Serra, the high metal walls of the Nautilus Dome wrapped around each other until reaching the Pearl Heart, a round room with rows of benches and an elevated platform in the center with four thrones for the Royal Family. During a recent refurbishment, Prince Moussa had added large LED screens, so that the Queen's face could be seen from any seat.

Everyone rose to stand when the Queen entered the Pearl Heart. She took her place on the High Throne and motioned for everyone to sit. Moussa, Oumar, and Ndeye took their places beside her.

"Good day to you, Stavros," Queen Awa called out.

"Your Highness," he replied. "May the Gracious Tides bless you."

Queen Awa chuckled. "No need for the formalities, old timer. Just call me Queen. We have known one another for many moons. Too many perhaps."

"How true," he blushed.

"Shall I guess the purpose of your visit?"

"I imagine you already know it."

She shrugged her shoulders and said, "Indeed I do. You would like our help with a man from Sicily."

"A Sicilian beast is a more apt description, I do believe. We were given a note that Gia passed to her attorney from captivity. Gia has a lawyer, Donatella Sapiente, who represents both Gia and the man who is holding her hostage, Quintilio Mosca. From information that

Signor Mosca told Donatella and from further information she gained from a confidential source inside his security team, she was also able to communicate to us his plans for Gia. He has built a large aquarium... he wants to lock her in it. It also appears that he is taking her on a trip across the globe to seize control of her empire."

Queen Awa's stomach flipped. "We cannot allow that." The thought of a mermaid being held in captivity was chilling. If it could be done to Gia, the most famous mermaid in the world, it could happen to any mermaid. Helping Gia was the right thing to do. Furthermore, Awa needed the capital from Gia's international outposts to fund her own ventures. "The note you have from Gia... what does it say?"

Stavros took the paper from his pocket and read aloud again. 'It says, 'Heed the warning of Laocoon when rolling metal horses are pregnant with water from the sea.' We are not sure of its meaning."

"My, my," the Queen chided, "do Greeks not know their own history? This is a rather obvious allusion to the Trojan Horse. My question is why are the horses metal in her riddle?"

Vittore raised his hand and spoke in his broken English. "I may speak?"

Stavros turned to him and spoke in Italian. "I will translate for you." So, Vittore proceeded to tell Stavros what needed to be said, and Stavros repeated it to the Queen. "Gia's lawyer told *Signor* Cantalupi that the aquarium is being filled with water trucks from all over Europe. This was the information that Donatella received, is that they drop the water off directly to the villa."

Queen Awa paused a moment and thought. "Rolling metal horses are the trucks," she deduced. "So, if a truck is a horse... and the warning from Laocoon was not to allow the wooden horse to enter Troy... because inside the horse were the Greeks, ready to battle... then she means for you to enter in the belly of the truck, which will be full of water from the sea."

Stavros's jaw dropped. "You are incredible!" He bowed down to her. "Queen Awa, the wise!"

"I do enjoy solving riddles," she smiled. Now, turning to the issue of who exactly will be swimming in those tanks... I am afraid I cannot commit my people unless you first ask Queen Zale to sanction the mission."

Stavros tugged on his beard and frowned. "We requested an audience with Queen Zale but have not yet received word from her."

"I see," Queen Awa sighed. "Then we have only one option, do we not? I shall have to accompany you there. According to the Pan-Atargatic treaty, she cannot refuse a face-to-face meeting with me."

"You would do this for us—for Gia?" Stavros asked, awed by her generosity.

"I have never been afraid of a little conflict with Zale. Our diplomatic party shall leave in five days' time."

Five days seemed like an eternity to Stavros, but they desperately needed the help from Queen Awa, so wait they must.

Awa leaned over to Moussa, covering her mouth and whispering in his ear. "Son, in the meantime, I want you to contact our friend in Paris, the one with the shipping company. Ask him to figure out where those water trucks are coming from... I want to know every detail he discovers."

38

January 14th

E ven on Q's fancy jet, the flight from Macau to South America was grueling. Adding three stops for refueling made the trip last for more than a day and a half. Plus, combined with jet lag, Gia felt woozy all the time. The baby seemed less active in her tummy, which worried her. More than anything, what Gia most longed for was a solid two days in her own bed in Venice and then a visit to the OBGYN in the Santorini colony. Neither were possible.

To make matters worse, for the last six days, Gia was once again the subject of an international manhunt—thanks to Harper. Because of this, Q was forced to reroute to Colombia, instead of heading directly to Argentina as planned. They hid out with a friend of his from the Medellin cartel. Apparently, after Gia's stunt in the Maldives, he preferred a land-locked location to limit his risk.

Their host was affable—as far as amoral narcos go.

Two days before, Gia had decided to change back into her charming mask of civility. She apologized to Q for her actions in the Maldives. Her efforts appeared to be making an impact.

Anxious to drain Gia's South American outposts of their cash, Q decided that it was time for a quick mission to Buenos Aires, then an even quicker jaunt to the Rio beach club. Facing mounting debts, Q felt he had no choice but to make the cash grabs.

Was it dangerous to tote Gia around with him?

Yeah, it was.

But at the same time, he didn't trust anyone enough to babysit her. And he certainly wasn't going to give up his infamous mermaid after the lengths he had gone thus far to capture her.

No way, she was his biggest prize to date, and he intended on keeping her for as long as he wanted.

So, Gia, the precious cargo that she was, had to be packed and transported wherever he went.

The night before they were set to leave the jungles of Colombia, Gia approached Q with a very enticing opportunity. When they were alone—not counting her two guards and his two—she tossed her long brown hair over her shoulder and got as close to him as she was allowed.

"Q," she whispered, "I want you to tie me up."

He narrowed his eyes quizzically.

"I think..." Gia summoned as much charisma as she could. "The problem is that we have been kept at arm's length. I know you are scared I will hurt you, but I promise you, I will not. There is too much at stake. I want to touch you, and I want you to touch me."

"Hmm," he closed his eyes as he mulled over her offer. Of course, he had already considered raping Gia, and the idea excited him, but what he preferred was for her to want him on her own, to ask for it—beg for it, even. He was quite pleased with her having come to this conclusion, before moving into the aquarium. It felt... *right* to him.

"Bring me some handcuffs," he barked to one of the guards.

For Gia's part, any leverage she could gain with him would be useful. Once she was in the bedroom, undressed and handcuffed behind her back, she fantasized about ways she might maneuver her way into slitting his throat and draining every once of his rotten blood from his dying body. Unfortunately for her, with the armed guards ever present, this was only a nonsensical daydream.

This was her life now: being locked at the center of Q's menagerie.

As she lowered her head between Q's legs and shut her eyes, she imagined that everything she was doing to him she was actually doing to Cameron. That way, when Q caressed her and kissed her, she was able to relax.

When his hand brushed over her stomach, she thought of the time that she and Cameron had made love in her plane on the way to New York. He had been so full of love for her and for their baby—a tiny seed just beginning to grow inside. The sweet memory of Cameron brought tears to her eyes, but she swallowed the pain, just as she swallowed when Q orgasmed.

* * *

THE FRIEND in Colombia loaned Q a jet. They touched down at a farm outside of the city and waited there. In Buenos Aires, a cartel henchman detonated a car bomb near Gia's club to divert the media and clear the area. Once Q got the signal, a caravan of SUVs motored into town and stopped a mile from her club. Gia was given a helmet and put on a motorcycle driven by Lorenzo. He handcuffed her to the seat, and tied himself to her with a bungee cord. They were waved past a cordoned-off area by a crooked cop.

She thought of bribing Lorenzo to let her go. But no amount of money would flip him, and she knew that.

What she did not know was that across from her club, Harper had a camera crew staked out. She gave them strict instructions not to leave under any circumstances, so they had neglected to vacate the scene when the police evacuated the area. The street remained under their watchful eyes.

As Gia and Lorenzo rounded the corner, she made an impulsive decision to throw her bodyweight in the direction of the turn. Doing so tipped Lorenzo's torso too far over, and he lost control of the bike.

The bungee cord that bound Lorenzo to Gia slipped and popped open. Lorenzo separated from Gia as the motorcycle spun out. Gia's helmet crashed against the ground, and she blacked out.

39

January 14th

"Oh my Gracious Tides!" Moussa whispered, nudging Oumar and shoving his cell phone toward his husband, "Look, look."

Oumar scrolled up and up on the screen. "What is all this?"

"Reddit conspiracy threads about Gia. She has broken the Internet! And this..." he clicked on a PDF to enlarge it, "is a toxicology report from Gia's dead boyfriend that got leaked."

"Which dead boyfriend?" Oumar laughed.

Moussa snickered. "I know that's right, *mon amour*. Gia *stays busy* killing. This is the American one... the Chris Hemsworth-looking himbo dumb-dumb."

"Chris Hemsworth? The man from *Jurassic Park*?"

"No, that's some other Chris... the Hemsworth one is in *Thor*."

"Ohhhhh," Oumar smiled. "He is fine."

Moussa punched his husband. "Uh-uh, no sir! You, *mon amour*, are a married man. But I will tell you one thing... Gia does not mess with ugly men."

"*Non!*" Oumar replied. "They must be rich. And they must be fine."

"Who could blame her! If you're gonna go through all the trouble, then... you might as well enjoy the process, right?"

Omuar shook his head, chuckling to himself.

Moussa continued. "These little Internet spy people in their mothers' basements are saying Gia didn't do the deed."

Stavros overheard the conversation and turned his head toward Moussa, "With all due respect, Prince Moussa, of course she did not."

"Mmmhmm," Moussa replied. "Whatever you say."

* * *

WITHOUT A DOUBT, never had so many mermaids boarded a commercial flight. Twenty-seven mermaids and one old human man on a small plane headed to Santorini... talk about breaking the Internet... that news would have been a nuclear-level explosion.

Vittore, along with Stavros and his family, made thirteen, and Queen Awa and the Senegalese delegation were a total of fifteen.

Once the diplomatic party got to the harbor in Santorini, Stavros borrowed a yacht from a rich buddy of his who parked it in a dry slip in the off-season. They boarded the ship and headed out to the Greek colony.

It was late afternoon when they arrived at Pearl Island. Golden sunlight radiated off the sand of the half-moon bay. The beach glimmered, and the crushed pearls in the sand reflected like tiny sequins.

Stavros helped Vittore suit up in scuba gear, and they descended, deep into the blue, with Stavros leading the way through the network of complicated underwater passageways. They emerged from the water, one by one, into the subaquatic village.

Moussa cast a sideways glance at Oumar, unimpressed with the Greek colony's natural beauty. Under his breath he muttered to his husband, "And *this* is supposed to be the financial hub of the Atargatic world? It feels like Lascaux... *prehistoric*. Desperately in need of a revamp."

Many of the others in the Senegalese party felt entirely the opposite way, finding the surroundings charming and otherworldly.

As all twenty-eight souls ambled down the main avenue, conversation in the shops and restaurants lulled. The Greek residents were absolutely stunned at the arrival of this large, uninvited group. Whispers began to swell.

"Who are they?"

"What is happening?"

"Is that Stavros?"

Stavros awkwardly acknowledged the chatter by nodding his head repeatedly, a wordless hello.

Queen Awa strode up to Stavros and Vittore. "I would like to go directly to the palace."

"Of course, Queen." Stavros took several steps back and let her lead the parade.

They took a left, and arrived at an archway five stories high. A large stone staircase led to a carved facade, ancient in its enormity. Vittore registered a sort of familiarity with the structure. He thought it looked quite a bit like Petra in Jordan—from the photos he'd seen at least, since he had never traveled much and certainly had not ventured as far as the Middle East.

The elaborate sculptures on the face of the palace told the story of the rise of Mermaids, the truth: All life is borne of the ocean. On either side of the palace were two chiseled waves, giving one the sense that a tsunami might wash it away like a sandcastle.

Oumar elbowed Moussa, "You cannot deny that this is beautiful, *mon amour.*"

"Would it kill them to add a little color? Just a splash of something to all this... this ruddy rock? If they painted everything black? Now... that would wow me."

Queen Awa glanced over her shoulder to chide her son, "Enough, Moussa. Stop with the snobbery and show a little respect."

"I am only sharing my opinion as a designer," he huffed.

Queen Awa reached the top of the stairs and lifted the large door knocker, a brass kraken with sprawling tentacles across the massive door.

The door creaked open, and a pair of white-haired women peeked out. They looked as old as moondust, ashen and drawn.

One spoke to Queen Awa in Atargatis. "Have you an invitation for entry?"

"Let Zale know that Queen Awa is here to meet with her. And please prepare rooms for myself and my guests."

The old women stepped aside and welcomed the party into the palace. Inside, the walls were rounded like a conch shell, and the coral-colored floor gleamed with light from the chandeliers above. The space was womb-like and warm. More palace workers appeared to show Queen Awa and Co. to their rooms.

Stavros took Vittore's hand as he was shown to his suite. Once inside, he closed the door and kissed Vittore.

"Have you been here before?" Vittore asked, steadying himself on the bed. The floor and ceiling of the suite were made of glass, which made him feel a bit dizzy.

"I poked my head through the front door once, when I was a boy."

"I wish I could have seen you as a boy."

"I feel the same, my young lover," Stavros replied, stroking Vittore's cheek.

THE FOLLOWING DAY, the party was invited to a banquet in the Great Hall. Everyone entered the room and took a seat at a long table. Queen Zale tiptoed in like a whisper. She wore a floor-length tunic, and her long hair was braided to one side. She wore a crown made of rope and seashells.

The two Queens bowed deeply to each other, and Zale took Awa by the arm before sitting.

Queen Awa spoke first, "I am here because one of your children needs your help. Gia Acquaviva needs her family."

Queen Zale shook her head, "She has chosen her punishment, chosen the clay over the sea. She has no family here. Not any longer."

Queen Awa considered these words and offered a thought-provoking response.

"Have you considered that perhaps it is safer to keep her close to you?"

"Our customs do not allow it," Queen Zale's voice, soft as ever, sounded like a light wind blowing sand along an empty beach.

"Then, I shall have no choice but to rally Senegal to Gia's aid."

"Doing so shall break the treaty between our nations. Dear Queen, I beg of you to consider our future... consider what may happen should you choose *enemies* over friends."

"I believe," Awa said, raising her head high, "that very soon we will need every Mermaid on Earth to address the challenges we surely must face. Gia is powerful. If given the proper training, I believe she could be a leader among leaders."

"Perhaps you have made your choice then?"

"Indeed it seems I have. Senegal stands with Gia."

"Then Senegal stands alone."

Queen Awa exhaled a deep breath before responding, "So be it. After our meal, we will depart."

"Should Stavros and his family choose to leave with you, then know that they will no longer be welcome here."

"Take heed, Queen Zale. Know that when a mother abandons her children, she steals their beating hearts and replaces them with stones. When many stones gather, an avalanche is inevitable."

40

December 1994

Gia's jacket blew open as she crossed the Ponte San Mosé. *How wonderful to be back in Venice after so long,* she thought, as the wind blew against her face.

She loved everything about the city, from the flooded bottom floors of the old *palazzos* to the pop-up holiday markets selling meat and cheese. And tonight was especially pleasing, because she'd invited Pierre to town for her birthday. She breezed into the Hotel Bauman early to survey the scene. Pierre was set to arrive in half an hour. She traversed the marble lobby and clacked her Prada heels down the corridor toward the back terrace.

As she pushed on the door to the terrace, a bartender called out to her, "*Mi scusi, signorina, ma la terrazza è chiusa.*"

The terrace, closed? This wasn't part of her plan.

Her mind turned through possibilities. Maybe she could tell the bartender that she suspected her boyfriend might propose, so she desperately needed access to the terrace in an hour or so. Then again, it would not be advisable to draw attention to being out there once she'd slit Pierre's throat, no matter how quickly she could ferry him down to her graveyard below. At some point the police would poke around—they always did.

What if the bartender remembered speaking with her? No, not a good idea.

Anyway there were three hundred bridges in Venice for God's sake. Surely she could manage diving off one of them with Pierre's limp body in tow?

It would be fine. She'd come up with a solution.

But what a boner-killer. Slashing through all the meaty little muscles in Pierre's neck was going to be her birthday present to herself. She resigned herself to the idea of not having her fantasy play out exactly the way she wanted it, out on the terrace of the Hotel Bauman as she'd imagined.

She shuffled back to the front of the hotel feeling shitty, slumping down into a velvet armchair. She ordered a dirty martini—filthy, with extra olives—and downed the whole thing in three tries, flagging the waiter to bring another, which she nursed more carefully.

The piano man played *The Girl from Ipanema*, and Gia frowned. How inappropriate a song for a windy December day in Venice. What hokey American had made that request?

The evening was already feeling tiresome when Pierre walked through the door with an ear-to-ear smile. Gia barely managed to look enthusiastic as she waved at her boyfriend.

He glided across the room and planted a kiss on her forehead. "I have brought you a surprise."

From the other direction, in came Florent.

"*Joyeux anniversaire, mademoiselle,*" he said, sipping from a high-ball glass.

Had they been here already? Why hadn't she seen them?

Gia said a sad, silent goodbye to the thought of murdering Pierre this evening.

"Ciao, Florent," she said, as they kissed on each cheek. His cologne was woodsy, and he smelled faintly of sweat. Gia felt a tingle at the nape of her neck as her mind flashed with the thought of him fucking her against a wall somewhere nearby.

"Oh, this will be a night filled with surprises!" Pierre squeezed Gia and kissed her.

"Really?" she bristled. "Do you have another child to introduce me to... a daughter perhaps?"

Her snark flew completely over Pierre's head. He was too focused on fiddling with something in his pocket.

Out came a little black velvet ring box.

A ring box!?

Florent took a seat across from Gia as Pierre continued standing. She felt her throat tighten, and tried to relax the muscles in her face in a way that made her look normal.

Pierre extended the box for her to take it. She accepted the offering as if being given a dead mouse.

When she opened it, she exhaled the breath she did not know she had been holding.

Thank God, she thought. *Not a ring.*

Instead, inside the box was a singular key on a silver ring that featured an Eiffel Tower bauble.

"I give to you the key—"

"—to your apartment in Paris. That is very kind, Pierre. Thank you."

"Yes, it is the key to the apartment... but—I was going to say, it is actually the key to my heart."

41

January 16th

Under the cover of night, just off the coast of Sicily, a matte black helicopter landed on top of a large yacht. Moments later, the ship's crew lowered a small speedboat into the surf. Down the service stairs on the yacht, two men toted a stretcher carrying Gia. They stepped off the boat and secured the stretcher in the back seat of the smaller vessel. Q and two of his guards slowly powered the boat toward land. Once they arrived, they loaded the stretcher into the back of a van and entered Q's estate through the side gate. Every step of their trip had been perfectly engineered to avoid any unwanted eyes. They slipped safely inside the villa like a dark fog on a black and moonless night.

* * *

"MY CONTACT HAS BEEN TRACING *Signor* Mosca's water trucks for the last eight days," Queen Awa explained.

Twenty-seven mermaids, Senegalese as well as Greek—Stavros and his family included—stood on their fifty-four legs around a table in one of the Coral Tower's many ballrooms. That particular ball-room had been commandeered to serve as a mission control for Project Goldfish, the name for which the unsanctioned rescue of Gia from Sicily had been coined.

And, of course, Vittore was there, deep in the sea below Dakar—although seated, not standing. Stavros had pulled a chair up to the table for him. Littering the surface of the table were important papers, like roadmaps and blueprints of Q's compound—as well as details about the sewer that ran below the property, and its path out to the sea.

"We must board the final three water trucks before nineteenth December," Awa continued.

From the stacks of papers, she fished out a large map of Europe.

"The first truck is coming from Marseilles, France. The second from Genoa, Italy. The third is being filled at this moment in Pula, Croatia. These three trucks will meet at the port of Naples on nine-teenth December. In Naples, all three trucks will drive aboard the last cargo ferry to Palermo just before midnight. This is our only window of opportunity... we must strike then."

She scribbled notes on a large sheet of blank paper.

"There is a shift change that happens at the port of Naples ten minutes before the cargo boat departs. New drivers will take over before making the eleven-hour ferry journey to Palermo."

On another piece of paper, she drew large Xs.

"We will split into three teams of nine. At the port of Naples, each group will sneak into the tank of their designated water truck. We only have seven minutes to slip into the tanks before the shift change ends, and the new drivers board the cargo ship."

Stavros tried to absorb everything Queen Awa laid out.

"How will we enter the water tanks?"

The Queen searched through her stacks of documentation until she found a drawing.

"Here look at this... we will enter through the hatch on the top of the tank. These steel hatches are designed to be wide enough to accommodate a man climbing in for cleanings. But first..." she pointed to a small valve on the side of the tank "...you must drain enough water to offset the weight of the nine of you. Otherwise, the water will splash out of the hatch on top, and you will not be able to get into the tank before the trucks board the ship."

Moussa tapped his foot over and over. "Mother, I'm not sure that seven minutes is enough time to drain the water."

"Seven minutes is all we have," she replied, firmly. "Once the ferry departs... after that eleven-hour trip... then the trucks will drive to *Signor* Mosca's villa, entering through the heavily guarded south-western gate." She shoved the map to the side and pointed to a diagram. "This is where we will breach *Signor* Mosca's lines of defense."

"And then what?" Moussa asked.

"Then we attack."

* * *

IN THEIR SUITE in the Coral Tower, Stavros and Vittore rested under the sheets, looking at the open ocean from their large-windowed wall.

Vittore laid his head on Stavros's hairy chest as his lover stroked Vittore's white hair.

"My young love," he said, finally, exhaling a heavy breath. "You must stay here in Dakar until we return with Gia."

"I will do no such thing," Vittore snapped back, withdrawing from Stavros.

"*Agapi mou*, you cannot make this trip. There is no scuba equipment big enough to allow you to stay underwater for eleven hours. You are a man, and Man is not meant for water. You would turn into a pickle if you were to be locked in with all of us inside that tank of salty water."

"I could come to the port of Naples and then meet you after in Sicily."

"Absolutely not," Stavros replied. "That is far too dangerous."

"Then I will come to Malta!" Vittore declared. "This is where everyone will go, once you have Gia, no? Lying here in Dakar like a fool... I will not do this. What if something happens to you?"

"I will be just fine. Do not worry your young little head about it."

"I hate this!" Vittore huffed, crossing his arms and leaning against the headboard.

"I will bring Gia back to you. I *promise*. Then we can all spend some time together, here in this beautiful place. Would you like that?"

Vittore frowned and pouted.

"Come here and kiss me you silly fool," Stavros said, tugging on Vittore's robe.

42

January 18th

Harper had been welcomed into LION's London office like an Olympian after a gold-medal race. Goldie Stern had taken the time to fly across the pond to introduce her to the staff. Harper was given a large dressing room next to the studio, which boasted an en suite bathroom and a comfortable lounging area, in addition to a hair and makeup station. Swanky accommodations, even if they were temporary. Harper relished being treated like the queen she knew she was, and her cardboard heart fluttered at the thought of what her New York dressing room might be like.

Someone knocked lightly at the door. Harper opened it to find a nervous-looking P.A. standing in front of her.

"Miss Langley, there's someone in the lobby to see you."

"I'm not expecting anyone."

"She's quite insistent that we bring her up. She says she's Gia Acquaviva's solicitor."

"Can you radio down there? I don't want to bring up some crazy person."

"Certainly." The P.A. whispered into their headset and then said, "They are putting her through to your phone."

Just then, the landline rang. Harper took it off its cradle and held it to her ear. "Hello?"

"*Signorina* Langley, my name is Donatella Sapiente, and I would like to share with you some information about my client that I believe you will find helpful."

"Who are you exactly?" Harper asked. "Gia's lawyer?"

"The one and the only," *La Nonna* laughed.

Harper clenched her jaw. "And how do I know you're telling the truth?"

"Because, *angioletta*, I know exactly what happened to your brother, and if you let me come up, I will tell you everything you need to know."

* * *

LION's NETWORK theme hummed as the lights of the London studio illuminated, and the main camera zeroed in on Harper's face, which was perfectly manicured for her prime time hour. Thanks to her coverage of Gia, Harper had managed to bump Monica Yung up to an earlier time slot, and Goldie Stern, of course, gave Harper all the runway she needed to take off.

"Good evening, LION viewers. Over the past week, you have watched as our competitor networks have tripped all over themselves, trying to locate Gia Acquaviva. I come to you tonight with a shocking report. *Truly shocking.* I can hardly believe it myself. Four days ago in Buenos Aires, there was a car bombing. We can tell you, exclusively, that the explosion was a diversion. Roll the tape, please."

There, on the screen, was slo-mo footage of Lorenzo and Gia on the motorcycle, coming down the street toward Gia's club in Buenos Aires. The bike swerved erratically and crashed, throwing Lorenzo onto the pavement. Gia landed onto the ground, too, but she was tossed off her seat, even as she was still handcuffed to the bike. The bike crushed her right arm.

The producer cut back to Harper. "Nasty fall. But, if you look closely at our *exclusive* footage, you will see something strange."

Harper rose to her feet and crossed the studio to a large monitor, playing the footage. She touched the screen and zoomed in on the bike. "The man here, seen driving the motorcycle, is Lorenzo Mosca. He is a member of a Sicilian crime family. That is not the strange part though."

She swiped over to Gia, zooming into her hands.

"Notice that Gia is *handcuffed* to the motorcycle. Handcuffed. And, there is a bungee cord tying her to Lorenzo." She turned to face the camera. "That means she wasn't riding on that bike voluntarily. Gia was in fact made a prisoner. And the question you are probably asking is *why*?"

Harper clicked around the monitor again and pulled up a mugshot of Lorenzo.

"This man, Lorenzo Mosca, has a very long criminal history. He grew up in Brooklyn, but about a year ago, he moved to Italy to work for this mob boss..."

Harper brought up an image of Q.

"Quintilio Mosca, a kingpin in the *Cosa Nostra* mob."

A dotted line extended out, and a photo of Gia popped up.

"What does this have to do with Gia Acquaviva, you may ask? Remember I said that the report I have is shocking? Here's where it gets complicated. I have an exclusive source close to Quintilio Mosca, who has revealed to me that it was actually *Mosca* who allegedly murdered my brother and *not* Gia Acquaviva."

Another two lines appeared below Q, one connected to a photo of Lorenzo, the other to a blank avatar.

"Lorenzo Mosca died in Buenos Aires shortly after this accident... but our source is very much alive."

She pointed to the empty avatar, a placeholder to keep *La Nonna's* identity secret, before swiping the screen, revealing a photo of Cameron. Below him, a timeline.

"December twentieth: my brother appears in Venice with Gia Acquaviva. Here is the security footage from that day." She clicked to enlarge it. "I can now confirm that the bones he is holding belong to the mother of Gia Acquaviva, Marina Acquaviva who was last seen in Monte Carlo in the 1980s. That's an entirely different story, so don't focus on that. Now, back to the timeline. That same day, December twentieth, my brother exits Gia's house, caught on camera by paparazzi and various news channels. After that he disappeared. My source revealed that he was kidnapped not far from Gia's house and flown to Quintilio Mosca's house in Sicily."

The timeline on the monitor extended out.

"December twenty-fourth... my brother's body is found in the canal. But you're probably wondering how I'm making the connection here, right? Well, there are two key pieces of information from my brother's autopsy report that make it clear to me that Quintilio Mosca is the alleged killer."

The monitor changed, to show a copy of the autopsy report, heavily redacted, with the key portions highlighted.

"This is a translated copy of the autopsy. One, they found a large amount of lemon pulp in my brother's stomach. Two, they discovered dirt under his nails that contained volcanic ash."

Harper swiped the screen again, this time showing a map of Sicily.

"This is Mount Etna. It's an active volcano in Sicily. And this... "

She zoomed in on the map, to an aerial view of Q's villa.

"...is Quintilio Mosca's compound, which also happens to be situated on a lemon orchard. Let's go back to the timeline. December twentieth, my brother was kidnapped, so between December twentieth and December twenty fourth, he was kept at this Sicilian megavilla, where he was fed lemons from the grove... and was likely held in some kind of room with a dirt floor, where he walked barefoot through soil heavily laden with volcanic ash."

She flicked back to Q.

"I feel confident in saying that Quintilio Mosca is holding Gia Acquaviva against her will. This is confirmed not only by the footage of her handcuffed to the motorcycle in Buenos Aires, but also by my anonymous source. Additionally, my team discovered that Gia was caught in the Maldives at the behest of Quintilio Mosca. *He* is the one we need. *He* is the one we're looking for now."

She enlarged Q's face on the monitor.

"Quintilio Mosca is at large. We need your help to find him. We still want to bring my brother's killer to justice. The network and my kind-hearted boss, Goldie Stern... we're upping the reward. One *million* dollars. That's right... one million dollars for the LION viewer who is able to aid in the capture of Quintilio Mosca."

43

February 1995

Gia and Dimitri cuddled in the hot tub on the roof of the Paris apartment. She'd come to town for the weekend to check in on the club. After the deed had been passed to Gia, she'd let Dimitri move in. After all, Pierre had his own apartment on the other side of town.

"Have you seen Pierre lately?" Gia asked.

"Just once... a few weeks ago. He popped by for an afternoon delight."

Gia's silverly-white tail bobbed in the bubbles next to Dimitri's, which was slick black. It felt so good to let loose together like this, to be merfolk. She flicked her tail and splashed him in the face.

"Afternoon delight! Hilarious. Better you than me. I am really rather tired of him... which is why I did not mention that I am in town."

"He seems off," Dimitri surmised.

"What do you mean?"

"Depressed."

"Really?" Gia leaned out of the hot tub, grabbing the open bottle and refilling their champagne glasses. "I cannot imagine Pierre as anything but perfectly sunny."

Dimitri shrugged, as if bored already with the examination of Pierre. "I forgot to tell you! Guess who came by last night?"

"I do not like guessing games, Dimitri," sighed Gia.

"Pierre's son. What a sex kitten, that one."

"Florent? Why was he here?"

"To pick up a CD for his father." Dimitri paused and then smirked in Gia's direction. "I did a bad thing."

Gia narrowed her eyes at him. "I just said I do not enjoy guessing games, so spit it out."

"I invited him over tonight."

She cursed at Dimitri in Greek. "You have ruined my evening. You do realize that?"

"I would not be so sure about that. Why don't we go get ourselves cleaned up before he comes over."

"You, *bello*," Gia grinned, pouring the last drips of champagne into her glass, "are far too filthy to ever be truly clean."

Dimitri's scales dissolved in patches, and then his tail evaporated into two strong legs. He hopped out of the hot tub and ran through the freezing air to the apartment below.

Gia stayed a while longer in the water, tail curved over the edge of the whirlpool, arms stretched out on either side. It was rather nice having an apartment in Paris.

* * *

CRUSHED ICE SWISHED in the cocktail shaker as Dimitri prepared cocktails for Gia and Florent.

Florent leaned against the kitchen island, staring at Gia without shame. Gia nibbled on an olive, looking in the opposite direction. Dimitri's eyes darted between the two of them.

Dimitri poured out three dirty martinis and distributed them to their owners. "So, um..." He found the vibe in the room awkward and in need of a shift. "Should we—"

"What exactly is going on between you and my father, Dimitri?"

"Pardon me?" Dimitri swallowed a sip of vodka, but it went down badly.

"Is he gay now? You *are* living here, right? Then I can only assume that you're lovers."

"Want to help me out here, Gia?" Dimitri said, bugging his eyes out at Gia.

Gia tossed her hair to the side and flipped toward Florent. "I do not like your tone, nor do I care for your homophobic subtext."

"Homophobic?" Florent balked. "What the fuck are you talking about? I'm bisexual."

"Oh, really?" Dimitri immediately forgot the awkwardness permeating the air and appeared to be practically jubilant.

Gia sipped on her martini, unbothered by Florent's attempts to gain attention. "Is that supposed to impress us, Florent?"

"I don't know, Gia. Does it?" he quipped.

With a bored sigh, Gia turned her attention to Dimitri, "Pass me a few more olives, please." Dimitri did as he was told, and then they all drifted into the living room, where Gia took a seat on the sofa.

Florent sat next, and then for a laugh, Dimitri plopped down in his lap. "Am I too heavy for you?" he asked.

"You're light as a feather," Florent replied, slapping Dimitri on his thigh. Dimitri let out a little cry. "Oh, do you like that?"

"Mmhmmm," Dimitri hummed.

Gia watched the boys, nursing her drink.

Dimitri rolled his eyes. "You're being very boring tonight, Gia."

She shrugged.

"I want to have some *funnnn*," Dimitri whined.

"Then you are in luck," Florent said, "because I have ecstasy in my pocket."

"Oooooh!" Dimitri smiled at Gia. "Can we, can we?"

"I am not your mother. Do as you please."

"What's wrong with you?" Dimitri asked. "Are you in a bad mood or something? It's really killing the mood, Gia."

Florent shifted Dimitri off of his lap and onto the couch. He reached in his pocket and pulled out three yellow pills. They looked like vitamins, and they were in the shape of a smiley face. Florent fed Dimitri one pill, and he gobbled it up. He scooted his way across the couch until he was right next to Gia.

"Come on," he said to her. "Let's have fun tonight."

"And if your father happens to stop by?"

"He won't. He's at a shareholder meeting or something... some kind of last-minute meeting about the sale of his company."

Strange, Gia thought. *Pierre did not mention anything about a shareholder meeting to me. That is rather uncharacteristic. Usually I cannot shut him up.*

"Do it, do it, do it!" Dimitri chanted.

Florent smiled at Gia. "Do you really want to spend the whole night watching us act like fools? Won't it be so much more entertaining to be a fool yourself."

"*Bene!* Enough. I give up."

The men cheered.

"Now," Gia said, "give me one of these pills."

After about twenty minutes, they were all rolling.

Dimitri played with Gia's hair, and it was the most relaxing, sensual feeling she'd ever experienced. Florent tilted Dimitri's head away from Gia and kissed him. Dimitri eased into the kiss and wrapped his arms around Florent. Gia watched them make out in front of her, and they seemed to vibrate with intense sexual energy. Her nipples got very hard. Hard enough that she felt them under her shirt, pressing against the fabric of her lace bra. She observed her chest moving up and down with every breath she took. Each time she inhaled and her nipples pressed harder against her clothes, she felt even more aroused.

She glanced over at the men again. Dimitri was biting Florent's neck, but Florent was looking directly at Gia. He wanted her, she could see that from how his eyes were narrowed and heavy. She had the strong urge to masturbate then and there.

But she didn't.

"I am going to lie down for a while," Gia said.

"Don't go," Dimitri begged.

"I will come back later."

Dimitri pouted. "At least give me a kiss before you leave, then."

She fumbled her way over to them, leaning in to kiss Dimitri. He put both hands on her cheeks, and when their lips touched, he used his tongue to open her mouth wider. His tongue tasted sweet, and she got lost in the feeling of pure sex. She felt Florent's face coming nearer to hers, and she opened her eyes. He was still staring at her, single-minded in his attempts to seduce her.

He pulled Dimitri's head back and went in to kiss Gia. She put her hand on his lips and stopped him.

"No," she said.

She rose and walked into her bedroom, locking the door behind her. She collapsed into the bed and imagined all the things that would have happened had she let Florent finish what she started. She took her time playing with herself. After quite a long time, she reached a satisfying—but somewhat lonely—orgasm.

44

Beep. *Beep. Beep. Beep.* The rhythm of an electronic bell punctured the thick, ghostly fog inside Gia's mind. As constant as a dripping faucet, she tried to place the noise.

An alarm clock?

The automatic alert a car makes when the keys are left in the ignition?

It sounded like the heartbeat of a robot. Before Gia could deduce the mystery, however, she was enveloped by the haze again and disappeared.

She flitted from dream to dream. Cameron cradled their baby. Then, they were skiing in St. Moritz. Later, they bathed in sunlight on a bed placed on top of a yacht.

Cameron whispered, "I love you so much. Let's name our little girl Serena. I've always loved that name."

There were nightmares, too, intense ones that she knew were—or could be—real.

In one, she woke up with her tail amputated. In another, she stumbled into a conference room, where all of her dead ex-lovers hovered around a table, grinning, necks gashed open.

"We've been waiting for you," they sang in unison.

The door slammed behind her and strong, male arms grabbed her.

"You would have killed me if you had half a chance." It was Cameron's voice, and he was full of anger and bitterness. He tried to strangle her.

That transported her right back to being fifteen on the boat in Monte Carlo, where her mother had died. The man who had gripped his hands around Marina's neck was now choking the life out of Gia, and she struggled to break free.

Her mother, head bloody and body limp, floated up beside them. She screeched, "There is a price to pay for all you have done. The Gracious Tides have turned to red, and they will take you under."

"Mamma, no! All of the bad things I have done, I did for you."

"I did not make you a killer, my daughter. You have a deep love of death and suffering. And you will be punished for it."

Gia shuddered at her mother's words. She felt ashamed, scared and unworthy of love. Darkness crept around her and suddenly she could see nothing. There was only a constant sound.

Beep. Beep. Beep. Beep.

The pulsating tone felt nearer now. Gia imagined it as a lighthouse and wondered whether she could steer herself into the harbor. She concentrated on the beats between the sound and pushed her mind ever closer to the edge of the fog. She became aware of people speaking around her and of her body—but she couldn't move.

The voices were garbled and distorted. She heard phrases as opposed to full sentences.

"Ultrasound."

"Not ready."

"Coma."

Coma?

That word zapped a jolt of adrenaline through her body and she felt something sticky and cold being wiped across her stomach. Then, gloved hands patted around and stuck her with some kind of plastic handle.

"Look," said a woman. "The baby is fine. Is it a baby? I guess it is. How strange to see a tail. This is incredible."

Gia put all of her energy toward opening her heavy eyelids.

"She is regaining consciousness."

Is this the same woman who was speaking or someone else?

Gia couldn't tell, even as she spied the brightest sliver of light between her thick black lashes. Everything seemed magnified—her lashes looked enormous, like they were under a microscope. She held her eyelids like that for quite some time, partly because she needed to adjust to the light, and partly because she didn't have the energy to open them all the way.

Someone leaned in. A familiar face, a kind one.

La Nonna.

"*Madonna!*" *La Nonna* screamed. "She has made it through." Then she began mumbling prayers and crossing herself.

"Where am I?" Gia grumbled.

From across the room, a voice boomed. "Back in Sicily at my house."

Gia recognized that voice. It was Q, horrible Q.

Gia whispered to *La Nonna*, "Do I still have my tail?"

"Ah, *angioletta*," she replied, wrapping her hand around Gia's, "you have two sexy little legs under this sheet, so I cannot imagine that your shining tail has vanished."

* * *

TWENTY FIVE MILLION tons of cargo move through the port in Naples each year. The massive network of buildings and docks employs nearly five-thousand people.

That day, as twenty-seven mermaids entered the port and made their way to varied sectors of the enormous structure—some to the cruise terminal, some to the shipyard, and others to the cargo loading deck—no one seemed suspicious. After all, one-hundred-and-seventy-five ships were set to pass in and out of the port on that day alone.

At eleven o'clock sharp, everyone reunited at the *rendezvous* point in the commercial section of the automobile terminal.

They hid in the back of a yellow shipping container marked "Bisset Industries." Most of the port had closed down for the night, but the automobile terminal was still humming with light activity.

The ferry would depart three minutes before midnight.

At eleven-thirty, the teams began to split off. Stavros led team A, Moussa controlled team B, and Queen Awa wrangled the final group, team C.

Moussa grabbed his mother for a sidebar conversation. "I feel like this is not my place, Mother. I'm not a fighter."

She widened her eyes at him, "My son is not a fighter? What are you saying? Moussa, if you are to take my place one day as the leader of our people, then you must stand beside them no matter what battles may come. Remember that kings who build palaces are toppled with ease, but hero kings collect hearts and rise."

"Really, Mother? Proverbs... *now*? I'm telling you that I don't think I can do this."

"You will do this, my son. You will do this, and we will be victorious. And when Gia Acquaviva comes to Dakar, you will rise up, and together, we will make Senegal the shining star of the Atargatic world."

Moussa swallowed. "You're right... you're right."

Queen Awa slapped her son on the back and then sent him on his way. He shuffled over to Oumar.

"Motivational speech?" Oumar asked, chuckling and stroking his chin beard.

"Do you believe in me?" Moussa asked.

"*Mon amour*," Oumar leaned in, embracing his husband, "I believe in you, I love you, and I hope that after tonight, you will finally believe in yourself. You are more than just a prince. You will be a king among kings."

Moussa leaned in, kissing Oumar deeply. "*Je t'aime*, Oumar."

Nearby, Queen Awa checked her watch. It was time to begin. "Team A, go!" Queen Awa whispered to Stavros.

In threes, Stavros and his team exited the shipping container.

After a few minutes, it was Moussa's turn.

"Team B, go!" Awa commanded.

Awa listened closely, there was nothing to indicate that things had gone awry. The captain of the cargo ship blew the horn, letting the dock workers know that it was ten minutes until loading time.

"Come, team, after me," Awa tiptoed out of the container and ran softly, hiding behind stacks of boxes as she made her way to Truck C. She peeked her head out and saw Stavros and Moussa's faces. The truck drivers were chatting with some sailors, smoking and drinking coffee. The shift was changing, and fresh drivers would take their place in only a few moments.

Queen Awa gave the signal, and she, Moussa, and Stavros each headed to the side of their respective trucks to begin seven minutes of draining. Moussa and Awa's trucks drained without incident. After a few minutes, they smuggled nine mermaids into Truck B and nine more into Truck C.

But Stavros had a serious problem. He couldn't get the faucet to turn. He waved over a grandchild who tried to open the valve—but to no avail. It was welded shut. They noticed then that a connector for a tube had been installed on the back of the truck, probably for faster draining. The problem was, that connector was locked, and they didn't have the key.

Stavros cursed under his breath as he huddled up with his team.

"There is only space for me in this tank. Contact Bisset at Bisset Industries for help. Meet us at the fishing ship in Malta."

As his team snuck away, Stavros climbed the ladder to the top of his truck, turned the wheel of the hatch, and dove into the saltwater.

45

February 1995

The dancers at La Perle Noire were dressed like the keys on a giant piano. Dimitri entered the stage in a coat with tails and took a running leap onto a sliding piano stool. As he tickled the girls, they each sang a note, and so the act became a sort of an *a cappella* jazz tune. It was definitely not Gia's favorite show-piece, and she made a mental note to tell Dimitri to kill the act and replace it with something more saucy.

Someone from behind placed their hands over her eyes, and Gia's gills instinctively fluttered into an active stance, ready to exit her fore-arms and slice on demand. She jerked the stranger's hands down and flipped around to see Florent's toothy grin.

"Don't worry," he crooned, "I didn't tell Papa you're in town. I wanted to see you again before you leave." He took a seat in the owner's booth next to her, sliding across the suede and putting his hand on her thigh. "We left things rather unfinished the other night, Gia."

"Yes, and there is a very good reason I stopped you from kissing me, Florent."

"I know you like me," he grinned. "I can feel it. I feel it even now." He leaned in closer and brushed her hair off her ears. "I bet you're wet. Aren't you?"

Gia held her breath just a little too long and gave herself away.

"Fucking knew it," Florent said. He moved his hand inside her skirt, and she let him. His fingers reached the edge of her silk panties, and she bit her lip to keep herself from making any sounds. He moved further, probing two fingers beneath her underwear, to find her glistening.

"Hmmm..." he said, mostly exhaling breathy tension. He slid his thumb in, and then quantified how wet she was by rubbing his thumb in circles on his forefinger. Grabbing a fist full of her hair with his other hand, he tugged her head to his face.

"I'm going to fuck you senseless, Gia. I don't care if you are my father's whore."

46

January 20th

Outside of Q's walled fortress, in front of the steel gates, the world's media had descended, and all were fighting for a prime strip of real estate. And crowds gathered, too, hungry to get in on the action and to witness the chaos.

Drones and helicopters buzzed above the compound while armed guards shot down any drone that succeeded in clearing the fence.

The scene that presented outside was so loud that it sounded like five simultaneous rock concerts were taking place. Sicilian police converged from all over the island, rushing to the madness and attempting to gain an illusion of control over the growing crowd.

Ashley Mason from OTN strutted over to Harper. "Hi stranger," she said, with a saccharine smile. "You have been so quiet since you left OTN."

"Quiet?" Harper scoffed. "That's hilarious, Ash. Everyone who is here right now is here because of *my* reporting. Including you. Quite literally, I *am* the news."

"Your parents send their regards."

"Really?" Harper smirked, looking away from Ashley and turning her attention back to the scene around them. "Be sure to give Royce and Bronwyn a *big hug* for me the next time you see them."

"I guess you must miss them a lot, huh? And the bigger audience at OTN," Ashley added, trying to crease her Botoxed forehead with *faux* concern.

Harper refused to take the bait, though.

"Ashley, I know it's really hard for a cute little girl from Kentucky to understand," Harper snapped, "but there are bigger and better things out there for me than my parents' shoddy network. My boss is Goldie Stern now. Did you know that he doesn't just own LION? That's cable television, sweetie...so people have to pay for it. He also owns a *network* station. People get those channels for free. People like free things. A free station means more people watch it. The trades are calling me the next Barbara Walters. Who knows... I might be hosting *The View* before it's all said and done."

Harper's LION producer started signaling to her that they were going to go live, so she swatted Ashley away like an annoying insect.

"I've got *work* to do, Ashley, so if I were you, I'd head back over to the OTN tent and start taking notes on how it's done."

47

March 1995

Inside Gia's Berlin club, house music throbbed like a beating heart. She'd been back in Germany for a week or so, ensuring that the milk was flowing smoothly from her little cash cow. When the bouncer knocked on her office door, Gia was lost in a stack of ledgers, crunching numbers.

"Someone's at the front for you, Gia."

"I am not expecting anyone."

"He says his name is Pierre."

Gia furrowed her brow. Pierre in Berlin?

"*Bene*, bring him down."

Within a few moments, Pierre was standing in her office, looking rather unlike himself, disheveled actually.

"*Amore!*" She kissed him. "Why are you in Berlin? Why not ring and tell me you were coming?"

"Do you have anything to drink down here?" He collapsed on a chair across from her desk.

She poured him a bourbon.

"What is the matter, *amore*?"

He downed the contents of his glass and took the bottle, pouring himself another. "My deal fell through."

"I do not understand what you mean."

"The acquisition. It is not happening. I started to worry in late January, because due diligence was taking longer than expected. I took out a loan to cover payroll last month."

"Oh, Pierre, I am so sorry."

"Gia, I need you to sign the apartment back over to me."

She shook her head, stunned. "I cannot do that, *amore*."

"You have to."

"No, I cannot do it... I already signed on the Amalfi property two weeks ago with Paris as collateral. The money has been transferred. I thought I told you that..."

"Perhaps you did. I have been so distracted, Gia," Pierre's eyes began to flutter and fill with tears. "I need your help. My line of credit is maximized, and I have to make payroll again. Could you—"

He couldn't bring himself to ask her, he was so ashamed. Pierre turned his head away from her and cried.

Gia closed the ledger and put it back under her desk in a safe, next to a stack of cash, locking both away.

"*Amore*, I am so sorry. I do not have a spare coin at the moment. All of my money is tied up, either in operations or in expansion. Could you ask your sister for a loan?"

"As if asking you was not humiliating enough. My sister will laugh in my face. I will have to sell the other apartment."

"There you go, Pierre," Gia said, encouragingly, "it is not so bad. You have options."

"Yes, but, you see, my ex-wife owns part of it, so it will not be enough. And you are sure, Gia... there is nothing you can do to help?"

"I wish I could, *amore*."

Gia wondered if her voice sounded sincere.

48

January 20th

"With all due respect, *Signor* Mosca. I cannot advise that you move her to the aquarium." Q's private surgeon stood at Gia's bedside doing his best to talk sense into his employer.

The head of security agreed with the doctor. "It is a security risk, sir. I think she is safer in the house. Especially with the crowds outside the gates."

"These are your *opinions*," Q spat, "and I have mine. Is the aquarium full?"

His head of security replied. "Almost, sir. The final water trucks are at the southwestern gate now."

"Let them in. I want Gia in that aquarium as soon as possible. Is that understood?"

Q wasn't stupid. He knew that with the media closing in, he'd have to abandon his cozy, feathered perch soon. He merely wanted the chance to realize his dream—to display his mermaid in her watery cage—even if only briefly. He hadn't come all this way and put all this effort into building the aquarium for nothing. Small men like these two could never understand how much it meant to him to watch Gia on the hill across the way, swimming in the moonlight. No one could have accomplished this feat except for him. Even if he ended up dying later, he imagined that he'd go down in the books as the boss who caught the biggest fish.

"But, sir," the doctor pleaded, "she is a long way from full recovery. Putting her in the tank… it is very dangerous. We need to monitor her vitals. I cannot be sure how her body will respond to the water. She might go into shock."

"Shock?" Q snorted. "She is a *mermaid*. They are biologically meant for the water. It will probably be better for her. I will not hear another word about it. Move her."

Gia didn't have the wherewithal to interject. Besides, it didn't matter. Ultimately, she knew that Q would do whatever the fuck he pleased with her.

Currently, one of her arms was strapped to the hospital bed. The other arm, which was broken and throbbing, was wrapped to her neck and shoulder. She knew it was futile to fight—she simply didn't have the strength. Gia promised herself that she would escape again somehow, once she felt better.

No one was coming to save her, of that she was sure. After nearly a month with Q, surely someone would have come already?

Perhaps *La Nonna* never gave the note to Vittore.

Maybe Q lied and killed Vittore anyway.

Gia clenched her jaw and squeezed her eyes shut, trying to quiet her rambling and anxious thoughts. When she opened them, a nurse was coming toward her with a syringe.

The needle punctured the skin on Gia's arm. She felt a fuzzy warmth tingle through her veins, and then she passed out.

Aided by the doctor and nursing staff, Q's guards loaded Gia onto a gurney and then moved her out onto the property. They crossed the lemon grove and arrived at the foot of the mountain. They unhooked the stretcher and carried her to a metal platform, riding on a scaffold to the top of the hill. The men toted her up a set of stairs to the very top of the aquarium.

They opened a door located on the ceiling of the aquarium and slid Gia's body into the water. She sank to the floor, coming to rest on a bed of seaweed.

* * *

AFTER THE WATER trucks spent some time waiting outside Q's compound, the guard finally waved the drivers through. Inside the metal tank on the truck, Stavros grasped onto the ladder. The past twelve hours had been miserable sloshing in the sea water all alone. He worried about the success of the mission. And there had been no time at the port to inform Queen Awa that things had not gone according to plan and that the team was now short eight merpeople, which had been central to their strategy. How could he regroup quickly enough to save Gia and smuggle her out?

There was so much noise outside, and he tried to discern what was happening. Sounds filtered through the water: helicopter blades whirring, people yelling. It was confusing, and in the dark tank, he felt like he was in an isolation chamber, far away from everything.

A few moments later the truck tilted up on a strong incline. The water in the tank crashed to the back and Stavros struggled to maintain his grip on the ladder. His tail swayed with the motion around him and he tried to remain focused as struggled to remember Queen Awa's plans step by step.

"At the top of the mountain is an access road to the aquarium. When the trucks stop, you, Moussa, and I will exit first and kill the drivers. Team A will slaughter every guard near the aquarium. Team B will run down the hill and secure our path to the sewer. Team C will fan out and get rid of any guard that comes near us."

Suddenly, the truck stopped.

Stavros waited for a moment for an indication of what was happening. Finally, he felt the front door of the truck slam. Springing to action, he climbed up the ladder and imagined that Moussa and Awa were doing the same in their trucks. He heard a loud banging on the outside of the truck as a tube was attached to it for draining.

That was his cue.

His tail dissolved into two legs and he unscrewed the hatch as quietly as he could, popping it open. He climbed onto the roof of the tank and slid down its rounded side, coming face to face with the stunned truck driver.

Before the driver could even scream, the gills in Stavros's arm shot out. He lifted his forearm and sliced the driver's neck wide open. Stavros covered the man's mouth and nose, hastening his death. As the man's body went limp, Stavros grabbed onto the man's torso and laid him gently on the ground. He then tip-toed to the back of the second truck.

Moussa was there, covered in blood and hyperventilating.

* * *

"I'm COMING to you live from Sicily," Harper shouted into her mic, trying to amplify her voice above the chaos around her. "Behind me is the compound of *Cosa Nostra* mobster, Quintilio Mosca. As you can see, masses of people are clamoring at the gates. The size of the crowd has been growing by the minute. It definitely feels as if this mob is about to get out of control."

The camera panned around to show the police struggling to push back an increasingly angry crowd. On top of the walls, guards remained vigilant, holding automatic weapons at the ready.

The camera operator returned the focus on Harper. "My brother's death has appeared to touch a nerve. People from all over Italy have descended upon this hilly and volcanic island, demanding an end to what they say are decades of corruption in the government and within the police force. In Italian, they are chanting, 'The police do dirty work... we want clean hands.' It's a tense scene that appears to be escalating. I encourage you not to change the channel. God only knows what will happen next."

* * *

Q WATCHED the madness unfolding from inside the walls of his mansion.

"Sir," the head of security said, rushing into the room, "we need to begin our emergency protocol."

Enraged, Q slammed his hand onto the coffee table. "Damn it! I am not ready to go!"

"But sir—"

"Out! I am not leaving yet. I call the shots here. I will call you when I am ready."

Q stared out, over the tops of his lemon trees, soaking in the view. Up on the hill, by the aquarium, the final water trucks had taken their places. However, he saw strange movements, which concerned him, but couldn't make out what was happening. He switched on the TV and flicked through the security cameras around the aquarium. He was not prepared for what he saw next.

A guard was attacked from behind, his throat cut.

Eyes wide, Q screamed for his security team.

* * *

MOUSSA WAS SHAKING. He'd never killed anyone before. It looked so easy in the movies. The good guys kill the bad guys, and everyone goes home happy. But now, with some poor man's blood all over him, he froze.

Suddenly, Stavros was there in front of him, saying something, but Moussa couldn't hear what. The air from the blades of the helicopter blew sand everywhere. Stavros grabbed Moussa's arm and dragged him to the back of Queen Awa's truck.

"Where is Oumar?" Queen Awa shouted.

Moussa pointed down the hill as Awa peered over the edge. Oumar had made it to the lemon grove. He was carrying a gun he took from one of the guards he killed.

"Come!" Awa waved for Stavros and Moussa to follow her.

* * *

HARPER INTENTLY EYED the crowd at the gate, excitement and antici-
pation surged through her veins. The police were quickly losing
control as the raging crowd grew. Harper had never done any
wartime reporting, but she imagined it felt much like this, just with
bombs dropping from the sky.

"Live in thirty seconds!" her producer yelled.

Suddenly, at the far edge of the police barricade, a woman broke
through the fences that had been lining the perimeter of the
compound, and a stream of protestors followed her.

"Live in five, four, three..."

"Harper Langley for LION. Here in Sicily, things are spiraling out
of control."

She had the camera operator turn the camera toward the crowd.
Her viewers bore witness to protestors who were now scaling the
walls. At the top, Q's guards opened fire, peppering bullets at the
would-be invaders, shooting several people unmercifully. Their
bodies fell backwards, landing on those behind them, and knocking
them down.

A horn blew several times. Someone shouted in Italian to clear
the crowd in front of the gate. Harper turned around quickly to see a
large bread truck barrelling in her direction.

"Move, move!" she frantically screamed at her crew. "Follow me!"
she commanded. Harper bobbed and ducked, the camera operator
followed in her wake.

The truck hit reverse, backed up, and then the driver pressed the
pedal to the metal and hit the gate full force. The driver died on
impact.

"OH MY GOD!" Harper cried. "What you've just witnessed is a
man trying to breach the front entrance of Quintilio Mosca's
compound, and as you can see, the force of the crash bent the doors
just enough to let people through."

The mob began running through the opening in the gate, their
screams of triumph and anger reached a fever pitch. Others climbed
on top of the bread truck and hopped onto the walls. Guards

peppered the crowd with bullets and shot whoever they could, but they were soon overtaken.

Harper squinted at the camera lens and bit her lip. "We're going in!"

* * *

Q's security team formed a circle around him and escorted him into the basement.

The head of security radioed for a status. "Front gate?"

"Front gate compromised," a guard responded.

"Retreat and activate emergency exit protocol."

"Affirmative, sir," the guard replied.

Q shouted at the head of security, "No! Send more men to the aquarium. Something is happening up there. I want it protected!"

The head of security shook his head in resignation and pushed the button on the walkie talkie. "Send five men to the northeastern hill."

"Copy that," the voice answered.

Q and his team came to the end of the hallway in the basement. The head of security pressed a remote control and the brick wall lowered, revealing the entrance to an underground parking lot. They dipped inside, boarded an armored Land Rover and set off into a tunnel that would empty them onto a nearby road through the mountains.

* * *

Stavros, Moussa, and Queen Awa arrived at the doorway to the aquarium.

It was locked.

Nearby, the body of a guard lay on the ground, lifeless. In a holster around his waist was a Glock. Awa spared no time retrieving it. She quickly removed the safety, aimed at the keypad, pulled the trigger, and fired several shots.

Nothing.

"Shoot the glass, Mother!" Moussa shrieked.

"I cannot, Son! The force of the water will break free and everything will wash out down the mountain, including Gia."

"Look!" Stavros bellowed, "The filter. Maybe we can climb in there!"

"But how will we get out?" Moussa screeched back.

"I will go in for Gia, you take the tube from the water truck. Use it to pull me out."

"Oh, help us, Gracious Tides," Moussa prayed under his breath before running to fetch the long tube.

Stavros tore off the filter, climbed in, and dropped into the aquarium. Queen Awa jumped in after him.

49

"I'm so nervous," Bronwyn declared as she smashed the elevator button with her car key and then slipped her keychain back into her Chanel bag.

The car dinged its way up to floor 101 as the Langleys were offered a view down to the footprint of the World Trade Center. It was equally dazzling as it was sobering. The ingenuity and brilliance of New York brought to ashes.

Royce recalled being further uptown at the OTN building on 9/11. Sad day.

But the 24-hour coverage that followed the attack changed the media landscape forever—and lined his pockets.

"Darling," Royce murmured, only half paying attention, "it's going to be all right. This guy is the best family lawyer in New York."

The doors glided open, revealing a marble lobby that featured a tall central wall engraved with a long list of attorneys' last names. A personal assistant appeared immediately to whisk the Langleys away to the VIP waiting room until the head honcho, the man with top billing on the letterhead, escorted them into his cavernous office.

The degree on the wall, from Harvard Law, read "Edward Ford Huntington, IV, *Magna Cum Laude*." There was an undergrad degree from Yale, also *Magna Cum Laude*. Around the degrees hung magazine covers featuring Mr. Huntington, Esq.'s long, narrow face and thinning grey hair under headlines like, "No Child Left Behind" and "The Top 20 Litigators in America."

"Coffee?" Huntington asked. His sunken cheeks and overall paleness belied a kind-hearted spirit—even if he was a bulldog in court.

Royce nodded. "Yes, please. Three sugars and half creamer. Vanilla if you have it."

"Diabetes," Bronwyn grunted to her husband under her breath.

Through stiffened lips Royce changed his order, "Three *artificial* sweeteners, please."

After the coffees arrived, Huntington whipped out a fresh yellow legal pad and slipped it into his leather-bound holder for active cases. "Let's dig in, shall we?"

Bronwyn began. "*Ahem..* you are likely aware of our son's passing. It has been chronicled extensively in the news."

"I have," Huntington replied, "and I'm very sorry for your loss."

"Initially," Bronwyn continued, "we thought it was his... the woman he was seeing... Gia Acquaviva." She paused and let out a frustrated sigh. "The... um... Mermaid, who was responsible for his murder"

"But she's not responsible?" Huntington asked, jotting notes on the paper.

"No," Royce jumped in, "we can't believe how this sounds when we say it... but... uh... it was a mob leader from the *Cosa Nostra* family. Sordid business. We still blame that Mermaid for getting him tied up in all this... this crap."

Bronwyn balled her fists in her lap and spoke, "We came to you because we are seeking custody of our grandchild."

"Gia Acquaviva's child?" the lawyer asked. Without moving a muscle in his face, he said, "And is this child also a... merm—ah... merperson?"

"We're not sure," Bronwyn responded, "but it's highly likely... given the mother."

"Understood," Huntington noted, still scribbling away. "Where is the mother now?"

Royce glanced over at his wife and frowned, "According to recent reports... it appears that she is being held against her will by that mob boss. She was recently involved in a motorcycle accident in Buenos Aires... but she was taken off the scene and has not been seen in days. We've called every hospital in South America... she's nowhere to be found."

"I see," Huntington hummed. "What day did the accident occur?"

"January fourteenth," Bronwyn replied.

"Have you considered... and I am sorry to have to ask this... but have you considered the possibility that she has lost the baby?"

Bronwyn cast her eyes down into her lap. "We're praying that's not the case."

Huntington nodded, "Of course, of course. And Ms. Acquaviva... does she reside in Italy?"

Bronwyn shook her head, yes.

"Do you have a residence in Italy?"

Royce and Bronwyn looked at each other, confused.

"Why?" Bronwyn asked. "Does that matter? Should we?"

"It would be much easier to obtain custody if your primary residence is in Italy."

"Italy?" Bronwyn scoffed. "No, no. We haven't the slightest inclination to move overseas. We want to raise the baby here and give her a proper upbringing."

"While I do understand," Huntington explained, "due to the Hague convention and an extensive and mounting volume of case law, removing children from Europe can be difficult... if not impossible."

"Impossible?" Royce huffed. "For two grand an hour, it seems like anything can be possible."

Bronwyn interjected, "This woman is an unfit mother! She's a criminal! A *nouveau riche*, trumped up club promoter! And she's a *fish* for Christ's sake! Even though she didn't kill our son, there's a body of evidence that she did kill her ex... ugh... lover. A Spanish movie star, no less!"

"That *is* helpful," Huntington replied. "But I will need to do some research. I can't say it will be easy... and unless she has been convicted of a crime, it's hard to say where the courts will land. Europe is... it's just a different animal entirely. So, I really don't want to get your hopes up. *If* Ms. Acquaviva survives and the baby is born... and *if* she puts up a fight... which I imagine she will... it seems as though she has the means to mount a defense... it's still an uphill battle. Also, have you considered how you might raise the child?"

"She'll have the best of everything, that's for sure," Royce bragged.

"Certainly," the lawyer noted. "However, what I mean is whether you feel totally equipped to raise a merperson?"

"How hard can it be?" Royce scoffed. "I won a goldfish once at the county fair!"

Bronwyn's face went blotchy. "I won't allow my grandchild to be raised by that psychopath mother of hers! Eating seaweed and bobbing around in the ocean? It's unimaginable, unthinkable! She needs a normal life with normal people!"

"I agree, my darling," Royce said, patting his wife on the leg.

"So what, then?" she yelled. "What is the plan, Royce?"

"Sweetheart," Royce raised her hand and kissed it. "Don't worry. We will figure something out."

50

January 21st

Gia laid on the floor of the aquarium looking pale and drawn—seemingly lifeless. Her tail didn't move. Stavros swam close to her to see if her gills palpitated, to see if she was breathing. Edging close to her, he finally saw the ruffling of the gills on her arms, and the tiny ones behind her ears took shuddering breaths.

She was alive, but barely.

Stavros lifted her by her shoulders as Queen Awa took her tail. Together, they carried her to the top of the aquarium, to the filter. Once at the top, Stavros tied the tube around Gia so she wouldn't fall down. He pumped his strong tail back and forth, rising high enough to take his head out of the water. Then, he tugged on the tube and Moussa ran over, extending his hand to help Stavros out.

From outside the tank, Stavros pulled on the tube, propelling Gia toward the surface. Awa held Gia's body, twisting her, so that she could fit through the opening. Stavros heaved with all of his might. Awa shoved Gia's tail, and together, they got her through the hole and out onto dry land.

"Stop right there!" a guard yelled in Italian.

* * *

LION's HELICOPTER hovered over Q's property, its camera aimed at the aquarium. The pilot radioed the ground team. "Get Harper up to the top of the hill! You're not gonna believe this! There are two merpeople trying to fish Gia Acquaviva out of this big tank!"

The producer answered back, "Are you rolling?"

"Hell yes!" the pilot whooped. "We're recording every second. Holy shit!"

* * *

OUMAR WAITED above the manhole that led to the sewer. Moussa, Stavros, and Awa were nowhere to be seen. In fact, he hadn't seen any of the troops who'd boarded with Stavros. Immediately, he feared the worst.

"I am going to find them," Oumar said. "If I am not back in fifteen minutes, come to the top of the mountain to find me."

He'd strapped a rifle that he'd lifted from one of the guards he killed when exiting the water truck to his back. Two other armed merpeople followed him. In the distance, Oumar observed a crowd of people spreading across the property like ants on the hunt. He hustled across the field of lemon trees, obscuring himself inside the foliage as he headed to the elevator on the scaffolding.

They ascended and found Moussa and Stavros standing, palms up as they faced five guards. Gia lay on the ground. Awa swished around inside the tank.

Oumar didn't flinch and reacted instantly. He began firing shots at the men who were threatening his husband. A guard in the back angled toward Oumar and returned fire.

One of the other merpeople with Moussa shot that man, and he fell to the ground in a pool of blood.

Oumar kept firing shots to clear the enemies. He was so focused on protecting Moussa that he did not see another guard far behind him.

The man popped into view, and Moussa shouted at Oumar.

"*Mon amour!* Take cover!"

But it was too late.

A bullet ripped through Oumar's right arm, knocking the gun from his hands. He collapsed onto his knees.

Moussa lunged forward to retrieve the gun, taking aim at the asshole who had shot his husband. He hit his target, and the guard toppled over.

Moussa rushed to his husband's side.

"Lie down, *mon amour*," he cried.

Oumar's hand was wrapped around his bicep, and blood leaked through his fingers. Moussa tore the shirt off a nearby guard and wrapped it around Oumar's arm. Oumar screamed in pain. "I have to press hard, Oumar. You have to stop bleeding so much."

Several members of her crew reached into the tank to help pull Queen Awa out.

* * *

"WE'RE in the midst of a raid on Quintilio Mosca's compound," Harper exclaimed breathlessly to the camera as she and the camera operator ran through the lemon grove. "We're going to cut to live footage from the helicopter." The producer switched the feed to the helicopter footage, as Harper narrated. "There appears to have been a shoot-out between Quintilio Mosca's security team and several... um... mermaids who have taken Gia Acquaviva out of a massive aquarium that looms over the property. Yes, what you are seeing is live footage of other mermaids, coming to the aid of the world's most famous mermaid, Gia Acquaviva."

The camera operator tripped and fell to the ground, but Harper kept talking into the mic. "We are making our way there now!"

* * *

"COME ON, COME ON!" Oumar commanded. "We have to leave now!"

The other mermaids helped lift Gia, and they all scurried down the hill and rode the elevator to the base of the mountain.

From the steel car, they could see that a wave of people were headed toward them—and at this point, the group did not know if they were friend or foe.

Moussa threw Oumar's arm over his shoulder, propping him up. Oumar was bleeding through two bullet wounds, and he murmured to his husband that he felt he might pass out soon.

When they reached the bottom, they sprinted as fast as they could across the property. Hundreds of people were right behind them. And one of those in pursuit was Harper Langley.

* * *

"JUST IN FRONT OF ME, there... that's Gia Acquaviva. She appears to be injured, and she's being carried by several people. We have confirmation that the white man with the grey beard is a mermaid, as well as the black woman with pink hair. We do not know the identities of these people... these mermaids."

Harper and the camera operator were jogging and nearly out of breath. But Harper was determined to get the story. No matter what it took.

* * *

STAVROS, Queen Awa, and the others made it to the outbuilding that housed the manhole that led to the sewer. The rest of the mermaids helped them get safely inside and then slammed the heavy door shut. Ripping the manhole open to expose their escape route, they dropped into the sewer one by one.

The crowd arrived at the door and banged on it, trying to get in. Three or four mermaids held them off, while Stavros and Queen Awa lowered Gia into the sewer.

Finally, the last mermaids dove into the manhole and shut the cover. The whole group swam through the network of pipes at top speed, headed toward the sea and the fishing boat that awaited them offshore. Queen Awa and Stavros held onto Gia's arms and propelled her through the water.

* * *

"THE MERMAIDS ARE BEHIND THIS DOOR," Harper shouted to the camera as the mob around her shoved on the metal door to the outbuilding, banging on it and kicking it.

After several minutes it gave way and broke open. Harper jumped up and down, trying to get a look inside.

Someone screamed in Italian, "No one is in there!"

Harper turned to a protestor and asked, "Excuse me, ma'am, do you speak English?"

"Yes."

"What did they say?"

"That the room is empty."

"Empty?" Harper asked, confused. "What?"

The woman shrugged impatiently and turned to head toward the main house, clearly on the hunt for new excitement.

Harper's eyes bore into the camera. "We're not sure what happened, but the mermaids seem to have disappeared. We'll be back after a quick commercial break."

After a few moments, the area cleared out and the mob dispersed, and Harper was able to get into the building. It was empty, just as everyone had said. But then she spotted the manhole and what had happened clicked into place in her mind.

"They've gone into the sewer," Harper whispered. "Fuck, we've lost them."

51

February 1st

Gia laid in bed as Vittore sat beside her. He stroked her head and spoke softly to her. "*Tesoro mio*, please, can I bring you something?"

Gia held one hand on her stomach, pleased to find that the baby's tail was tickling her inside even though her body still felt mangled. And her mind was just as wrecked. She jumped at the slightest noise, which made sense. It had been less than two weeks since she'd been put to sleep in Sicily and woke up on a fishing boat headed for Malta. The trip back to Senegal hadn't been an easy one either.

Stavros gently rapped on the door and entered Gia's suite at the Coral Tower. "It is time." Stavros helped Vittore off the bed.

Both men wore white suits.

"Do you feel well enough to come to Oumar's funeral?" Stavros asked Gia.

She didn't answer as she felt a twinge in her chest.

Guilt, perhaps?

"Maybe it is better for my *bella sirena* to rest," Vittore sighed. However, his words made Gia finally snap to attention.

"Do not call me that!" Gia demanded. It made her think of Q. "Never call me that. Not ever again." She struggled to pull herself up off the bed and Stavros and Vittore jumped forward to steady her. "Help me into that dress, please."

Later, the three winded their way through the Nautilus Dome. Mourners chanted sea whispers and songs of the dead in Atargatis. The voices splashed off the curved metal walls of the Dome and washed over Gia.

Inside she felt a dark, infinite hole expanding within her. She imagined Cameron and Oumar falling through it. In the bottomless pit of her soul, she felt that she might destroy everyone and every-thing. Part of her wanted to. But then she thought of Q, and she shivered.

Are we the same, he and I? she wondered, confusion rife in her head. *Do I take so much pleasure in the pain of others? Surely not.*

She felt no pleasure now. Only bleakness and sorrow. Pain welled up inside her, filling her up until she was overcome, at last it spilled out. She wailed.

Stavros held her up.

In the Pearl Heart, Oumar's body was laid out on the round plat-form. Around him burned a thousand candles. Under him was a woven bed of coral and turquoise beads in the pattern of a nautical star.

Moussa kneeled at his husband's feet, weeping. Queen Awa embraced her son's shoulders from behind, steadying him. She wore a white robe and a crown made of shells and pearls. She looked like Yemaya incarnate.

The funeral parade took their seats, and Awa helped her son as he left his vigil next to Oumar and made his way to his seat.

Finally, Awa straightened herself and raised her head to begin the ceremony.

"O Gracious Tides, bless those who suffer. Wrap us in the wave of your love and carry away our pain. Scatter our sorrow to the currents and wash it away. This we whisper to you."

She glanced out among the familiar faces of her people and those belonging to visitors from other nations: Stavros and his family, Gia and Vittore, and leaders from Brazil and the Arctic Circle.

"Let us sing the song of sorrowful hearts," Queen Awa commanded. Then, a chorus of voices in harmony rang out in the cathedral.

> *Life begins as life ends.*
> *We, the children of the sea,*
> *await the day the Tides ascend.*
>
> *Rise child, rise and see*
> *such beautiful waves at ease.*
> *Lift our hearts and pass the key.*
>
> *Our dark days soon will leave.*
> *Moonlit dreams will come once more.*
> *Atargatic reign begins this eve.*

After much prayer and many songs, Oumar's body was lifted and taken out to the sea. Vittore stayed inside and watched the merfolk swim away.

Not far from the Coral Tower, the funeral procession reached the resting place of the dead. A group of mourners tied Oumar's body to the seafloor. Moussa laid the first stone, placing it on his husband's chest, near his heart.

One by one, the funeral party arranged stones until Oumar's body was totally covered.

Queen Awa laid her hands on Oumar's grave, blessing it.

52

February 14th

Q had stolen so much from Gia, but at least he had not taken her jet. Securing her freedom had felt impossible only weeks ago, so boarding a plane at this moment brought Gia a thrill that she had never before experienced—regardless of the destination. She had been home in Venice for only a few days when *La Nonna* called her with an invitation to attend Cameron's memorial on behalf of the Langleys.

Still recovering from her injuries, Gia wore a cast on her broken arm. The pain that throbbed throughout her whole body was intense, but she was determined to make the trip to New York.

Everywhere she went now, she traveled with security. No, it was not enjoyable for her, but considering Q was still out there somewhere—not to mention the fact that she was now an international celebrity—Gia knew her safety required backup, the professional kind. She begrudgingly hired a four-man team.

Stavros dropped Vittore off at the airport to meet Gia and kissed his lover goodbye as they turned their attention to New York.

Gia and her party boarded the plane very early in the morning.

She wanted to get stateside as early as possible to beat the impending blizzard that was about to hit the east coast. Gia watched the sunrise from inside the plane and stared out the window for a long time, hours maybe. She thought of Oumar's funeral, and how he'd sacrificed his life to save hers. She recalled the mere months she had had with Cameron. Deep regret blew through her hollow chest.

The grief of losing Cameron sometimes felt too painful to bear. Something inside her ached enough that she was certain it must be heartbreak—if indeed she had a heart to break.

Gia had never loved a man. Cameron had been the first.

"*Methusalamme*," she said, reaching out for Vittore's hand,"do you think Cameron and Oumar are the price to pay for everything I have done?"

"*Tesoro mio*, I prayed to our Father in the Sky for him to protect you... and he did. I cannot think that his only goal is to punish you."

She lowered her voice to a whisper, "You do not know all the things I have done."

"Tell me. Unburden yourself," Vittore urged her, his voice comforting her.

She closed her eyes and shook her head. She would never tell him the whole truth. If he knew about all of the murders, it would be impossible for Vittore to see her the same way. How could he?

Furthermore, on close internal examination she couldn't say she regretted killing all those men. The contrary, actually; the eroticism of ending those lives excited her. She would do it all again if she could.

Femme fatale, damsel in distress, expectant mother, grief-striken lover... Gia was not able to wrestle control over all the dissonant identities and related emotions bumping against each other in her head.

"Do you think I will ever love again?" she asked Vittore, trying not to cry.

After all the horror and the trauma Q had put her through, Gia was sure now that she could have tamed her darker urges and found happiness with Cameron. He was the star of all her dreams at night and the fuel for her reveries in daylight. If anyone could have broken her habits, it had been him.

"Ahhh, but of course you will," Vittore replied, his eyes turning up at the corners. "This *sirenetta* inside you is coming, and we will both love her... and she will love us back. And as for a man... I do hope you will find love. You deserve someone who loves you as I do."

"Maybe I deserve to be alone," Gia said, turning her head to the window.

"Bah! Nonsense. Everyone has darkness inside, Gia, even an old man like myself. What? You think I have been an angel all my life. Absolutely not. Our Father in the Sky has forgiven me many times, yet I continue to disappoint him. Am I less worthy of love? I think not. It may have taken a long time for me to find someone, but I have been blessed with Stavros."

"Everyone who gets close to me dies."

Vittore reached out and tenderly touched her cheek. "Look at me, *tesoro mio*." She faced him. He gazed at her with deep love. "You have suffered terribly. You lost your sweet mother so young... and then your father too soon after. I have always loved you like my own, and I will love you from beyond the grave. Do not see yourself as the monster under the bed. The true monster is your grief. I know this. Maybe your grief has led you to make certain choices... but in my heart and mind, I know that there is goodness in you. I refuse to leave this world until you are able to see yourself as I see you. I love you, Gia... and you are worthy of my love and so much more."

* * *

THE PLANE SHOOK as it hit a stretch of turbulence during the final descent into New York. The tops of the buildings were covered in thick, pinkish fog. Gia had rented a Mercedes van to transport herself, Vittore, and security to the church in the Hudson Valley where the service would be held. She wore a black shift dress to hide her pregnant belly and a black fur coat. A choker with a long string of black pearls hung down her chest.

The Langleys had erected a perimeter around St. Margaret's Cathedral. As expected, the scene was a zoo. News crews had taken over the ritzy hamlet.

And why wouldn't they?

Certainly they all hoped to catch footage of the famous mermaid, Gia Acquaviva... but more than that, there were celebrities, heads of state, and titans of finance. All wanted to curry favor with Royce by putting in facetime at the memorial.

Being at the center of a tragedy had done wonders for Royce's reputation. Everyone was eager to do deals with him again. They felt he was the access point to something special. Additionally, amongst members of the inner circle, Harper's move to LION was viewed as tasteless and disloyal. She'd won over the fans but lost the establishment.

No matter, Harper intended to use the memorial as an opportunity to cement her status in the upper echelon, but she was entirely unaware that she was unwelcome there.

As for the presence of Gia, yes, they had invited her, but they had an ulterior motive. Royce and Bronwyn had serious business to discuss with her, and Cam's memorial was the perfect lure. When they left word of the invitation with *La Nonna*, they simply asked that Gia not cause a scene. But Gia had no intention of doing so; she merely wanted closure.

Gia's driver parked by the side entrance to the church. She and Vittore were flanked by her security team and ushered into the second pew, sitting directly behind Royce and Bronwyn. Gia couldn't remember the last time she'd been into a church. It was definitely her first time in an Episcopal setting.

Huge photos of Cameron lined the sanctuary. In the center of the aisles, where his coffin should have been, stood a simple, silver urn holding his cremains.

The service began and the clergymen led prayers. Cameron's friends read scriptures. Finally, it was time for the finale, the eulogy, a duty Harper had claimed. She rose from her parents' pew and strode up the aisle to the pulpit. She didn't need a script. She'd already burned into her mind what she wanted to say.

As she adjusted the microphone, she scanned the audience—some faces she recognized, others she didn't..

And then she saw Gia.

Their eyes locked on each other, and Harper had the strangest feeling: She felt connected to Gia, drawn to her.

Harper cleared her throat and spoke.

"Though most people would never believe it, my brother and I had a normal childhood. We hid in the treehouse in the backyard and pretended to be on a desert island. Years later, we hid in the tree-house for a different reason—my brother got me drunk for the first time. I was fifteen, and he was already twenty-one. He told me that he wanted me to be able to hold my liquor, because men are pigs, and he didn't want anyone taking advantage of his little sister. He was my protector.

"He was a respectable rebel... when he chose to go into banking instead of news, I think it broke my father's heart a little. But no one could stay mad at Cam-Cam. He was light and warm... he was as I tried to be... however, I failed.

"You all know me as the hard-hitting, shrewd woman on your TV screens. I promise you... that version of me annoyed my brother very much. He brought out a softer side in me that... if I'm being honest... I'm afraid it might be lost forever. Everything we have been through in the past few months has been unimaginably hard. You watched me say and do things I never imagined I would. But that is all right... I can forgive myself because all I was ever doing was acting out of love for my brother.

"Was I wrong? Yes, I was. If you will notice, Gia Acquaviva is here today."

Harper paused as she watched heads turn in Gia's direction.

Gia felt the hot glare of hundreds of eyes on her.

I do not think I will ever get used to this attention, Gia thought. *What I would not give to return to anonymity. Why is Harper putting the spotlight on me? What is she planning?*

"Gia is not my enemy. She will be the mother of my niece, and we intend to let bygones be bygones and accept her as part of the family."

Not an enemy? I am now, in fact, "part of the family?" Gia straightened her back, trying her best not to look as though she was reacting to anything Harper was saying. *Did she obtain her parents' approval to say that?*

"We all have our sweet memories of Cameron... and our stories that we will share and laugh about... and cry. But Gia carries with her the future of Cameron Charles Langley... his daughter."

Do you not mean my daughter, Harper? Cameron is gone. This baby now belongs only to me. Gia placed her hands on her belly, instinctively protecting the child within.

Harper dabbed at her eye with a handkerchief before continuing the eulogy. "So, you see, while we are still reeling from the grief and the anger over losing Cameron in the prime of his life, we have hope for a future to come. And... I believe that is what my brother would want.

"Here's to hope. I love you, Cam."

* * *

As Gia left the church, snow fell from the sky like powdered sugar through a sifter. Gia's driver followed the parade of cars to the Langley's manor. When they arrived, Gia and Vittore huddled in a corner of the expansive mansion behind her security guards and ate canapés.

No one came to bother her, and she suffered no unneeded attention. All the mourners were focused on Cameron's family.

However, as the crowd dwindled, and the chatter softened, Bronwyn came for Gia and beckoned her forward with her finger. Gia tapped the guards on the shoulders, and they parted.

"Let's speak in private, dear," Bronwyn purred.

Gia's head of security winced, but Gia patted him on the hand and said, "Don't worry, you can wait outside the door."

"Grab your coat, Gia," Bronwyn said, "we're going to my office."

Gia wrapped herself up and trailed Bronwyn through the snow to her cottage. Two bodyguards checked the perimeter and then stationed themselves at the front door to the building.

Royce was already inside snacking on a hidden plate of catering when the ladies walked in. Gia noted Harper's absence.

"Have a seat, please." Royce gestured toward the couch, and Gia took her place. Royce and Bronwyn sat down in two armchairs.

Bronwyn leaned in and began, "We only know some of what you have been through, Gia, and what we do know is harrowing. The unpleasantness between us is in the past. When we discovered that you did not k—"

Bronwyn couldn't bring herself to say the words, so Royce picked up where his wife had left off. "Gia, once we realized that you did not take our son's life, our only concern was for your safety and for the safety of our grandchild."

Gia tensed.

Did she believe them? Hell no.

Was she going to go along with the charade? Absolutely.

"Thank you," she sighed. "Your concern for me warms my heart."

Royce took his reading glasses out of his suit jacket and put them on. "We have something for you." He pulled open the side table's drawer and took out a file, which he opened. "Mr. Quintilio Mosca... fifty-eight years old. A leader in *Cosa Nostra.*" Royce peered over the edges of his glasses to see Gia's face twisted into a frown. "I'm guessing, darling, that you would give just about anything to get your hands on this son of a bitch."

"That is true," Gia replied.

"I have good news for you," Royce said, eyebrows lifting. "We have him,"

Gia felt her heart pump faster, breath clenched in panic. "What do you mean you *have* him?"

"He is in a secure location," Bronwyn chirped.

Gia's eyes darted back and forth between the couple.

"Your lawyer," Royce grumbled, "Donatella Sapienti... she has been so very helpful in all of this."

Gia's shoulders had started to shake, and she couldn't stop them. All that she had been through once again rose to the surface of her memory, and anxiety and panic exploded inside her. "I do not understand."

Bronwyn scooted over to the couch to sit next to Gia. "As long as he is alive," Bronwyn cooed, "you will never feel safe. And the thing is... we can't hold onto him forever."

Royce jumped in, "What Bronwyn and I are offering you is... well... freedom."

Gia's teeth were chattering now. It was all coming back... her escape in the Maldives... the dangerous sex with Q... the accident. She hugged the cast on her arm to try and soothe herself.

Royce came over to the sofa, sitting down on the other side of Gia. He whispered, "We can get you alone in a room with him tonight. He won't be able to hurt you, he won't even be able to touch you, but you can do whatever... and I mean *whatever* you want to him."

"That's right," Bronwyn explained, really selling it. "If it's revenge you want, you can have it." She paused to take in Gia's demeanor, and the woman was clearly in crisis. Perfect, Gia was exactly where Bronwyn wanted her to be. "In exchange, we just want one thing from you."

"What?" Gia asked, voice trembling.

Bronwyn reached over and pulled out a contract from the file and handed it to Gia. Bronwyn's eyes, cold as the Arctic tundra, were fixed on Gia. "We want custody of Cameron's child."

53

May 1995

Dimitri and Florent took turns sniffing lines of coke off the coffee table. Gia wasn't one for cocaine, so she hung off to the side, watching the boys do their thing. She'd flown into Paris for the day, as a quick stopover before heading to Amalfi to set up the new club for the busy season.

She popped Madonna's *Erotica* CD into the sound system before unzipping her dress all the way down the front, stepping out of it, and laying it on the sofa. All that was left on her body was a bra, a garter belt, and her heels.

"Crawl over here," Florent growled. She bent over slowly, so the men could get the full show on the way down. Then she wagged her tail like a kitty and pranced over to them on her hands and knees. Florent lifted her onto the coffee table and spread her legs. "Kiss her Dimitri," Florent ordered.

"You do not need to ask me twice, little sir."

Florent slapped Dimitri across the face, "Don't call me little. Open your mouth." Dimitri did as he was told. Florent unzipped his pants and got up on his knees. His cock was a bit soft due to the coke, but

Dimitri took it in his mouth willfully, which helped stiffen things up a bit. Satisfied that he was now hard, Florent shoved Dimitri's head between Gia's legs. While Dimitri went down on Gia, Florent took Dimitri's pants off.

Standing back for a second as a bystander, Florent watched his lovers. Gia ran her hands through Dimitri's silky hair as she glanced over at Florent, who was stroking himself.

She motioned for him to come over, and he did.

She took his cock in her mouth, and when he was super hard, Florent walked over and lifted Dimitri by his hips. He spat in his hand to lubricate entry and put just the tip of himself inside Dimitri. He eased in deeper, leaning over to kiss Dimitri's shoulders.

"Dimitri," Gia said, lifting his head, "I want you inside me."

The men moved together, slowly, so that Florent remained inside Dimitri. Then Dimitri pulled Gia down to the edge of the coffee table and pressed himself inside her. It felt so good to be full with Florent from behind and thrusting into Gia at the same time. All three were totally focused on their own pleasure, but also aware of the intense feelings of the others, which heightened the experience.

As such, not one of them even noticed when the front door opened and Pierre stepped into the living room.

Pierre's mind immediately dissolved into confusion, borderline sensory overload.

The scene was too much for him to take in. Pierre swayed in place, unable to move or scream or to do anything really. He had the feeling of being in a waking nightmare, and his legs went wobbly.

Florent craned his neck over Dimitri's shoulder to look at Gia, but instead glimpsed his father standing behind the sofa, only a few meters away.

"*Oh, poutain!*" Florent cursed to himself, pulling out of Dimitri. "*C'est Papa!*" He slapped Dimitri on the ass to get him out of the way and grabbed a sofa cushion to cover himself up.

Gia shot up off the coffee table to face her boyfriend. "Pierre?!"

Pierre's skin was grey, his mouth sagged and askew as if he had just experienced a stroke. He steadied himself on the back of the sofa to keep from collapsing. On the floor in front of him, Dimitri and Florent scrambled to throw their clothes back on. Pierre squeezed his eyes shut very tightly, as if doing so would erase all he'd seen. He shook his head violently, rage beginning to bubble up.

"Papa," Florent approached his father timidly, "let me explain—"

"Explain what?" Pierre said, fists balling. "Do not further humiliate me by lying to my face about what I have just witnessed with my own two eyes. I know what I saw!"

"*Bene*," Gia said, steeling herself, "you are right. There is no need for fiction here." She walked to the wet bar to pour whiskey into two crystal tumblers. She gulped heartily from her glass and pressed the other out toward Pierre. He glared at her, unable to hide his disgust, and snatched the tumbler, chucking it against the wall. It shattered into nearly as many pieces as his heart had.

"My own son, Gia?" Pierre spoke through gritted teeth. He threw his hands over his face to mask his shame. "I am a fool. I thought you loved me." His voice cracked, and he tried as best as he could not to cry, which caused his shoulders to shake violently. "I thought th— that we had a future... I..."

Pierre dropped his hands and turned his head toward the door to the terrace, absently shuffling outside.

Gia, Dimitri, and Florent exchanged wary glances, unsure of what to do. Dimitri plunged down into the couch and rested his head in his hands, silently wishing he could leave this new threesome to deal with their own problems.

Florent stared at Gia, "For fuck's sake, Gia! Go after him."

"You are the one who started this," she replied, coolly.

"You really are a cold-hearted cunt."

Florent glanced out the window to see his father balancing on the edge of the balcony's wall, head cast down to the street, many floors below. Florent sprinted outside, "Papa, come down from there."

Pierre muttered to himself, "I am totally alone."

Gia walked toward the wall, intent on pulling Pierre off the ledge. "Please, *amore*, stop this. I am sure we can talk about this and come to some resolution."

"Ha," Pierre let out a breathy laugh. "Resolution?" When Gia was within inches of Pierre, he screamed at her, "Get away from me! I do not want you here."

"Papa!" Florent was desperate now. "I'm sorry! Please, come here. Step down."

"My son," Pierre cried, "do you know that I have not one cent to my name? Worse than that, I owe money I cannot pay. I am worth more to you dead than alive."

"That is not true, Papa! I love you!"

"And you fucked the woman I love! You betrayed me! You have all betrayed me!"

"Pierre," Gia said, voice perfectly calm, "I have something very important to tell you. But I need you to come down first."

Pierre slid on his heels, turning to face them both, still teetering on the wall. "Why should I believe anything you say? Everything that comes out of your mouth is a lie."

"I will give you back the apartment, Pierre," Gia pleaded. "And I have money set aside from Berlin and the casino in Venice..."

"You what?" Pierre screamed. "Now you have money!? So you *lied to me* when I asked for your help?"

She lowered her head.

"I could kill you!" Pierre lifted his foot to leap off the ledge toward Gia, but his back foot slipped and instead of falling forward, he fell backward. He tried to grab the edge of the wall as he tumbled down, but it was all in vain.

Pierre careened down, down, down, until his body landed in a thud, spreading itself across Avenue George V.

54

February 14th

Not one iota of light filtered in through Q's blindfold. The ball gag holding his mouth open made it feel like his jaw would never be able to fit back in its socket. He'd lost feeling in his hands from the zip ties long ago. The IV drip in his arm stung, but he was more upset that he had to piss his pants when he needed to go. He was exhausted and angry—and lacking enough self awareness that it didn't even dawn on him that his current situation might be due to karma. Where was he and who had him?

The last day he remembered had been a Thursday.

How long had it been since then?

He had been sleeping peacefully at a friend's hacienda in rural Mexico, feeling as if his immediate troubles that he had experienced in Sicily were behind him, when he was taken in the dark at gunpoint. He never even saw a face. There was no time to call out for help. He was trapped like a snake in a bag, and there was nothing he could do about it.

He'd been thrown on a plane––to who the hell knows where. No one spoke... not a word, which was so strange. He hadn't heard a sound in days. He almost wondered if he'd lost his hearing. All that was around him was blackness and pain.

He occupied his time flipping through a mental rolodex of grievances. Who'd done this? Obviously this was a mob job, but whose? Russia? China? Surely not Colombia or Mexico. He had always done his best to build strong bonds with fellow kingpins.

He hadn't been tortured, so maybe this was a ransom situation. But wouldn't someone shove a camera in his face or cut off a finger or something?

The whole thing felt off. And that is what unsettled him. This is not how he would have done business, that's for sure.

Then he heard something... the clanging of metal, very heavy metal, like the door of a shipping container being opened. This was followed with the sound of soft footsteps crunching on the floor. Someone tore off his blindfold, and harsh light beat down on him. A flashlight. He jammed his eyelids shut and turned his head. He felt blinded, assaulted by red, muscly blasts of light.

Then the light switched off.

"*Buona sera*, you motherfucker."

It was Gia.

She tore off his ball gag next.

"*Bella sirena*," his mouth was like two sheets of sandpaper rubbing against each other.

Strangely, he never considered Gia as a possible kidnapper. How could she ever get access to him? This kind of operation was way above her pay grade.

"Look at me," she screeched.

He tried, but he could barely see her.

Gia felt rage rising inside her. She'd never killed anyone for revenge before. It definitely did not feel like the other times, but she did find herself beginning to get aroused. On her right forearm, her skin split apart as her sharp gil emerged. It was good that she only needed one gill to slash him, since her other arm was still lame from her time with Q.

Approaching him slowly, so he could begin to fear what was coming, she began on his shoulder with a tiny little gash.

Q screamed hysterically but she laughed, "That is *nothing!*"

Then she zig-zagged across his arm, cutting him deeply. He wailed, and the more he vocalized his pain, the deeper she cut. She shone the flashlight down to watch him bleed. There was so much blood from so many cuts.

It is incredible that humans contain this much liquid.

"How do you feel now Q, being at the wrong end of torture? I can only imagine all the things you must have done to people over the years."

She dragged the serrated edge of her gill across his chest. A bubbling waterfall of blood followed. He was crying out for his mamma now.

Good, this is what he deserves.

She lifted his head and stared into his soulless eyes as tears leaked down his cheeks.

"This is for killing the only man I ever loved."

She lifted her arm above her head and struck downward across his neck. It exploded.

Leaning against the padded wall, Gia watched him bleed to death. When he finally stopped convulsing, she was panting and very aroused. She would remember every detail of this kill for the rest of her life.

55

July 21st

"Hee hee, huuu huuuuuuu," Vittore made ridiculous breathing sounds as if he was trying to mimic the lead actress in an 80s movie featuring a teenage pregnancy.

"*Fermata!*" Gia cursed, bouncing her hands off the baby pool in her living room. "That is ridiculous, and it does not help with the pain!"

The old man paced up and down, up and down the hallway. Vittore's anxiety radiated throughout the room—and it was annoying Gia.

"If you continue to carry on this way, please, just go to the barber shop. I will do this on my own!" Gia screamed. Her eyes were wild and her wet hair flayed around her shoulders in heavy chunks—she channeled a pregnant Medusa.

"I will not leave, *tesoro mio!* Not for all the money in the world would I go from here without first holding my *sirenetta*. You made this old man wait until his eighties before having a grandchild, and then you tell him to behave. No, no. Absolutely not."

Gia threw her head back and rested it on the edge of the pool. "Fine!"

The OBGYN had flown from the Greek colony to help with the birth.

It took a hefty sum to entice her, but the doctor took the money and lied to her colleagues about a conference at NYU, slipping out of Greece in secret.

Gia was not interested in doulas or midwives. She wanted a proper doctor present, even if this was going to be an at-home water birth. Furthermore, with a baby mermaid on the way, this birth required a specific kind of expertise.

Finally, after ten hours of grueling labor, out came baby Serena.

Everything about her was normal: her weight, her length, her ten tiny fingers.

And her tail? It was golden and soft.

The baby was blonde haired and blue eyed, just like her daddy had been. She opened those big blue eyes under the water and kicked her tail.

Then, when the doctor gave the go-ahead, Gia scooped her daughter out of the water and held her in her arms against her chest. Vittore sat in a chair beside them, beaming. He wiped tears away with his sleeve.

"Father in the Sky!" he cried. "Never have I been so happy." He caressed Gia's head with one hand and the baby's with the other. "Pleasure to meet you, *sirenetta*. I am your *nonno*."

Gia squeezed her baby and breathed in her essence. "Welcome to the world, my little Serena Francesca." Gia thought Serena smelled like the clean sea on a cloudless day. The doctor applied a few drips from a bottle onto the baby's tongue, and the scales on her tail dissolved into two string bean legs.

"She is too skinny, *tesoro mio*," Vittore said, holding onto Serena's ankle. "We will feed you lots of milk, *sirenetta*... and when you grow in the months to come, you can chew some nice lobster."

Gia shot a glare at Vittore, and he giggled.

"Only teasing, *sirenetta*. For you, Serena, we will find the best gnocchi in Italy!"

Suddenly, they heard shouting in the front courtyard as someone pounded on the front gate. Gia's head of security rushed outside to check on the guards stationed at the front. He left one man guarding Gia.

What is happening? Gia felt her heart thud with worry. *Why must there always be trouble? Am I not allowed one perfect moment without interruption?*

The doctor helped Vittore out of his chair and he wobbled to the front door to see what all the commotion was about.

"Police! Open the gate!"

"I have instructions to keep this gate closed!" The head of security shouted back. "A woman has just had a baby, and she is resting! Now have some decency and go!"

Outside, camera crews stationed in the canal alongside paparazzi rolled footage on every bit of action. This had become Gia's norm.

Il Capo banged on the door and slammed what appeared to be an arrest warrant up to the aperture for the head of security to see. "Open this door," *Il Capo* commanded, "or we will come in using force."

"One moment, please." The head of security returned to the living room to inform Gia of the presence of the police, and their official orders to enter the premises.

"Open the gate as they have asked," Gia sighed, kissing her baby on the head. She glanced over at Vittore, who was nervously shifting in his chair. "Here, take her." Gia passed him the baby and struggled her way out of the birthing pool.

"Where are you going?" Vittore demanded. "You just had a baby!"

"Away. If they are here to arrest me, I cannot stay. I refuse to be locked up again. I will have *La Nonna* call you as soon as I find safe harbor." Gia scurried out of the front door and slid into the pool without a splash, turning the lever to the underwater hatch at the base of the pool and exiting into the canal. She zipped under the press boats and whipped around a corner without being detected.

The police marched through the courtyard and burst into the living room. *Il Capo* slammed his boots down at the edge of Vittore's chair. "We have come for the baby," he said, shoving a judge's order under Vittore's nose.

Just then, through the foyer, breezed another set of wretched figures.

Royce and Bronwyn entered the living room, smiling ear to ear, like two rotten American Rumpelstiltskins. Bronwyn shot over to the baby and stretched out her arms.

"Come to Grandmother Brownie, my darling."

Vittore held the baby tightly with both arms, refusing to give her away.

"Go on, old man! Hand her over!" *Il Capo* shouted.

"No!"

"You must!" *Il Capo* commanded.

Vittore began to tremble, and tears fell from his milky eyes. He looked down at his granddaughter and spoke to her softly. "*Sirenetta*, I will be with you again soon. I promise you this. Your *nonno* loves you so very much. Your mamma and I will find a way to bring you home. Now, here is your *nonna*." He wrapped the baby in a blanket and passed her to Bronwyn. "Be careful with Serena Francesca."

"Hello, little angel." Bronwyn hugged the baby to her chest. She rubbed Serena's cheek with her forefinger while gazing down at the baby's blue eyes, and found herself choking up. "Hello Serena." She looked over at her husband. "She looks just like Cam-Cam." Royce's mouth scrunched up; it was the only way that he could avoid bursting into tears.

Bronwyn turned her attention back to Serena—all of the other commotion in the room forgotten.

"Sweetheart, you're coming with us to your new home in New York."

56

EPILOGUE

"Park Avenue?" Gia spoke to her real estate broker over her cell, standing in an airplane hangar outside of Paris. "Four bedrooms? No. I told you six bedrooms at a minimum. I need a room for my daughter and space for my security staff. I do not care what the price is. Find me the biggest, safest apartment in Manhattan." She hung up and slipped the phone in her bag, pulling her hat lower on her head.

Her security team had ensured that there was no press around and that no one was taking photos, but Gia was becoming increasingly paranoid, and fame was not her forte.

Scanning the space, she was relieved to see that there was only one other jet in the hangar, a smaller one. On the fin of that smaller plane was a logo and the words, "Bisset Industries."

But Gia didn't notice.

Her thoughts were occupied with her journey to New York—and her ensuing custody battle for Serena.

It wasn't until she saw a face from the past descending the airsteps from the other plane that she snapped out of her rumination, and was brought back firmly into the present.

"*Bonjour*, Gia," the man said, sauntering straight up to her. Her security guards formed a protective circle around her, but she waved them away.

Squinting her eyes as if not believing what she was seeing in front of her, she whispered, "Florent, is that you?"

"Gia," he winked, "you have not aged a day."

IF YOU LOVED THIS...

Love this book? Leave a review!

Dying to know what's next for Gia?
Pre-order the next book in the series today!

ALSO BY JINCEY LUMPKIN

Mermaid of Venice (English language version)

Sirena de Venecia (Spanish language version)

Mermaid of Sicily (Coming September 20, 2021)

Mermaid of New York (February 2022)

Mermaid of Paris (May 2022)

Mermaid of St. Moritz (September 2022)

Mermaid of Monte Carlo (December 2022)

Made in the USA
Middletown, DE
23 August 2021